TALES OF BART
A Novel in Three Acts

TALES OF BART
A Novel in Three Acts

JOSÉ ALANIZ

A Flowersong Press Imprint
McAllen, Texas

A FlowerSong Press Imprint
McAllen, Texas

Bless thee, Bottom! bless thee! thou art translated.

— Shakespeare, *A Midsummer Night's Dream*

When I could give him not one minute more and the place had emptied but

for his lone awkward figure, planted there, overfilling the seat with its big

black bulk, resolutely ignoring my calls from the bar for the last quarter of

an hour, it was then that I approached the man's table, making as much

noise as I could, from behind his back.

"We're closed. Time to go. Disappear."

For most drunks these three terse sentences are enough, but he proved

to belong to that minority of Parisian drunkards who require their more

forceful, at least more forthright, elaboration. I sat myself down at his

table, the apron on my lap, to more closely scrutinize

this stranger who six hours ago had sat down, uttered a single

word, "Brandy," and had thenceforth occupied himself with but two

activities – one intermittent, the other as constant as the flow of the street

crowd outside the plate-glass window.

The former involved the flicking of a finger to indicate his wish to have

the glass refilled – by now his flicks had consumed nearly an entire bottle

of Bramartine – while the latter consisted of a steady, (I would even say

preternatural) fixation on the brown paper package lying on the table

before him. It appeared so ordinary as to arouse unease.

"Monsieur," I said in an even tone. "By day I study philology at one of

our sterling capital's less fashionable institutions. Truth to tell, the subject

does not fascinate me in the least. However, commitments are

commitments, certainly in my father's eyes if not in mine. That being the case, I am compelled to proceed home forthwith, after I lock up this establishment, which comes after you vacate your fat ass out of this seat, pay your tab and stagger out of here. You will understand that neither you nor the hour inspire a subtler approach."

I noticed that at the word, "philology," his heavy black lids had blinked. And had I been in the proper mood to appreciate this, I might have seen that the darkened ambience of the bar after I'd extinguished most of the lamps did lend his silhouette a near-menacing aspect, like a mountain in clouded moonlight. He certainly cut a notable if disheveled figure in this touristy part of the Latin quarter near the Pantheon: a heavy-set negro with oily curls, an almost regal slouch, lips that protruded like fat grapes on a dewy vine, sweaty skin of deep shimmering obsidian. These features were the extent of what the available light, spilling from the boulevard, afforded my vision. But no, I was not in a mood to appreciate any of these incidentals, and as my patience ticked away with the seconds, and still no response was forthcoming from this smelly boor, my body tensed as I weighed my options, finally braced itself to stand up and walk over to the phone.

"I am a translator," the man said.

Something in his utterance, I cannot explain what, froze me to my chair, in sudden expectation, though of what I could not fix either. The figure slowly swiveled its head, its twin black eyeballs, to me.

"I am Bart."

"Barthes?"

"Non, non. I am not some simpering critic caring for his terminal mother and ruminating on polaroids. There is no pleasure in my text, I assure you. And my camera is most definitely obscura. My name is Bart."

I was either in the presence of a madman, or perhaps merely a drunken fool. Yet his peculiar manner, perhaps the influence of the dim light, or the affected speech, set him instantly apart from the usual species of drunkard with which I nightly enjoy congress. For one thing, I could not place his accent, though I did decide his French, however flawless, could not have been Parisian.

"In exactly five minutes," the man again abruptly changed aspect, turning back to his former object of attention, "two men will demand to be let into the bar. They will ask for a person fitting my description. I would be more than happy to greet them – this was, in fact, the arrangement – but I fear my bladder can hardly hold out the long seconds 'til that anxious rendezvous."

I stared at him, striving to make out in that newly soporofic and slurring profile, some hint of genuine emotion, some sign of connection to this world.

"You will help me, will you not, my young friend? Inform these kind gentlemen that I've stepped into that tiny roomlet with a piss-covered hole in the floor you French call a toilet, and if they so wish, I shall happily and with open arms receive them there."

It was a scene out of Balzac, or a parody of such, if you like. This burly Algerian lout was wasting my time, setting me up for the ridiculous role of concierge to his doubtless equally besotted companions. The memory of whatever had struck me about this character instantly vanished, replaced by a scowl.

"You can hold your rendezvous outside, monsieur. I have no qualms of calling –"

But he was already heaving his huge toad's frame from the table. His fine but unkempt clothing emitted a fresh stench. I found it, strangely, a bit unnerving to see him move so quickly from his perch after having lain there all but motionless an entire evening. It was as if one of Rodin's misshapen monstrosities had suddenly sprung to unwieldy life.

His face still swallowing the light, he towered over me, though not an unusually tall man. He seemed and acted, in point of fact, quite pathetic, yet again some inscrutable facet of his person pinned me anew to the seat. He leaned with both arms on the table, which shifted under his weight, at last looking me full in the face.

"I remind you, my linguist friend, that the letter Beta started out as a shelter," he said, breath indescribably awful. Though he addressed me, he seemed to be speaking more to himself. "A place of sanctuary which the Greeks stole from the Phoenicians and in which we, by countless accidents and misdirected wills, have wound up taking refuge. Moved in to an abandoned house bequeathed us. Yet our inheritance, like all such *birthrights, is grossly, grievously undeserved. By rights we should all be languishing, howling with our fools in the pitiless storm … Christ, I'm pissssssed!"*

He disengaged, nearly lost his footing, chuckling as drunks do, and started retreating to the loo.

"Ah, well. My vstretimsya pod stolom, as the Russians put it, eh, lad?"

He froze in mid-sway, turned once more back in my direction. "Do be a good lad and do as I asked. And my effects there," he pointed shakily to the package, "do take care of them. Keep them warm, and so forth."

And he disappeared into the hall.

Not more than a minute could have elapsed before Bart's prediction came to pass. They were two well-dressed men – white – whose loathsome accents and pathetic French immediately betrayed them as Americans. Tapping on the glass, they seemed oddly tense; one would gaze quickly about the thinning street while the other focused on obtaining ingress. But then two very strange things occurred.

First: the men quickly grew agitated when I refused them entrance and demanded they await their friend outside; he would be coming forthwith. I too was getting quite incensed at the inconvenience to my own schedule. When the object of our impatience stubbornly failed to emerge, I was finally forced to walk to the back and wrench him, if necessary with my bare hands, out of the pisser and out of the bar and out of my life forever. When angry pounding on the door in the narrow passageway proved fruitless, I concluded with gritted teeth that the decrepit boor must have fallen asleep inside, and swiftly opened the door with my key.

There was no one in the loo.

A quick search of the premises by all three of us confirmed we were the only living souls present. And yet this was clearly impossible: the only other exit was a back delivery door, which had been locked three days and appeared untouched. And how could the windowless, subterranean loo have remained locked from the inside with no one in it? I had clearly heard, in the brief interval before the new arrivals, the drunk whose acquaintance I had just struck loudly urinating in the toilet, and bawling out some song in a language I didn't recognize. Then my attention was distracted by the figures at the door, and that was the last I had heard from Monsieur Bart.

The two newcomers were frantic. Oddly, they never suspected me as an accomplice in any mischief; they seemed to already know I was uninvolved. When their friend – though from this pair's behavior the accuracy of that epithet was growing more dubious by the second – could not be conjured, they shifted their aim to locating some object they would not name but eagerly sought out under tables, in trashcans, even behind the counter.

Enough was enough, and I ordered them gone. This bizarre end to my shift had swallowed up too much time and good humor and they could all go hang for all I cared. The Americans stormed out the front door, frustrated, evidently torn between some mysterious need for secrecy and the agonizing temptation to interrogate me in detail about what I had or hadn't seen. "Shhhhhit. He did it again," I heard one of them spit out in their guttural tongue before they vanished into the night.

At last, loudly slapping my hands, I turned to the final particulars of the evening. Within five minutes I'd put key to lock for the last time and was trundling home in a light drizzle.

At my apartment in the eighth arrondissement, near the university, I performed in reverse several of the tasks I'd just assayed at the bar: unlocked, undressed, switched on, set to boil.

I left the shades in place.

Soon, by the light of a small lamp, I sat in the living room before the coffee table, the cup steaming in its accustomed corner. Bart's package lay before me.

The second very strange thing: just before the Americans had first pressed their handsome faces to the glass, some impulse I could not explain led me to pick up the paper parcel within the folds of my apron, out of sight. At the loo, once I ascertained the negro was indeed gone, I deposited my unknown prize in the most surreptitious spot – down my shorts. I have been called skinny by some; the combination of loose pants and covering apron formed the perfect, bulgeless niche for the flat object wrapped in paper. Keep his effects warm, Bart had said.

Now I opened the thing. As I suspected: manuscripts.

An odd and eclectic assortment. The documents seemed to hail from different ages: some crisply laser-printed, glossy white, others typed, or handwritten, still others yellowed and fragile with age, newspaper clippings attached – some of the clippings themselves at the verge of transmuting to dust. A smell of ashes and years permeated the texts. One actually looked singed, blackened at the edges.

I deemed it a fair exchange. The author, after all, had left his evening's tab unpaid.

Carefully, I picked up the first manuscript, on top of the pile, kept together, and apart from the others, by a rubber band.

Settling back in the couch, I opened the first page and began to read …

El Gregín

*Being an Agony in Thirteen Bits
with Commentary*

...
3) A translation should read like an original work.
4) A translation should read like a translation.
...
9) A translation may add or omit from the original.
10) A translation may never add or omit from the original.

— Theodore Savory, The Art of Translation

He was Ahriman. He was Loki. He was Lucifer and Set. He was the bad god, cast in awful flesh.

— Alan Moore, Miracleman

For the Snark *was* a Boojum, you see.

— Lewis Carroll, The Hunting of the Snark

Bruce

Oct. 25, 1985

From: Bruce Vasquez, Texas Senator
        State Capitol Building 00788, Rm. 42
        Austin, Texas 78956-9888

To: Raul Robledo, executive director, Navarro Family Archives
        3 Plaza de Biliardos
        143700 Mexico, D. F.

RE: J.B.Vasquez Testimonial

Dear Señor:

Buenós Dias, amigo! I take time out of my hectic schedule to request yet again from you a copy of the Vasquez testimonial (1863) in your holdings. I reiterate that it has tremendous personal importance for me. As a boy my grandfather Abel would regale me with stories about my famous abolitionist ancestor, fighting the good fight down there in the old country. It was these stories, I can tell you, señor, that inspried me to seek public office and fight for civil rights in the first place. So you can undestand why I would really like to see this document, which you say is so obscure and unimportant, though I can't see why. Frankly, I find your resistance to my request a little strange.

Surely rehabilitating this story about my great-great grandfather's time spent in Texas, right in that time between free republic and statehood, would be a great way to celebrate the upcoming Texas Sesquicentennial. We have lots of things planned for the event, and if you could get me a copy of the originl document soon, I could have my staff translate it for release in the summer of next year, when many of the festivities will take place. We invite you, of course, amigo!

In fact, I've had it in mind that publishing the Testimonial around Juneteenth, since it deals with a theme related to slavery/emancipation and the black community, would be a great way to promote Solidarity amongst all minorities. It could have truly lasting and profound effect on our relations. On a personal note, I understand that great-great-great grandpa Vasquez (ha ha!) wanted this particular piece to be read by future generations of the family, and once it's translated for me I intend to do just that!

So please, Señor Robledo, whatever your objections to the document (if it's a bit antiquated or needs polishing up for publication) , speed it over to us and we'll give it the best treatment. You have my word. I eagerly look forward to the piece.

                                        Muchós Gracias,
                                        B. Vasquez, Sen.

December 27, 1985

From: Bruce Vasquez, Texas Senator
      State Capitol Building 00788, Rm. 42
      Austin, Texas 78956-9888

To: Raul Robledo, executive director, Navarro Family Archives
      3 Plaza de Biliardos
      143700 Mexico, D. F.

RE: J.B.Vasquez Testimonial

Señor:

Just wanted to say a big Texas GRACIAS!! for finally getting me the copy of the Spanish testimonial . It took a while, but we got it here now. Like I wrote before, I'm sure your objections to it, whatever they were, were just a little stage shyness. I looked over the original language, and it looks real nice and poetic. "Querida patria, mi luz de esperanza!" Gorgeous. We're having it translated now so I'll be able to appreciate the full effect. Again thank you and expect your invitation to our Juneteenth gala on Burnet Plaza very, very soon.

Sincerely,
B. Vasquez, Sen.

February 1, 1986

From: Bruce Vasquez, Texas Senator
State Capitol Building 00788, Rm. 42
Austin, Texas 78956-9888

To: Raul Robledo, executive director, Navarro Family Archives
3 Plaza de Biliardos
143700 Mexico, D. F.

RE: J.B.Vasquez Testimonial

Señor:

I order you, I demand that you destroy the original manuscript. of the V. testimonial immediately. If you do not, I will urge my cousin Abram Navarro y Quesada in Mexico City to ask for your swift resignation. You are a

I will not say what you are. you lied to me. you have caused a scandal here in the senate. I had that thing photocopied and sent out to 20 members of the Juneteenth planning committee!

Destroy that thing in your holdings. I don not care what it atkes. That man was no relative of mine.

B. Vasquez, Sen.

PS. You arew not invited to anything

Bernabé

My Testimony

attested to by Juan Bernabé Vásquez y Navarro
(gentleman, publisher, former privy councilor to the Minister of State, *amicus
humani generis* & Agitator for the Cause),
freely given under the eyes of God
this 28th day of October, 1863 *anno domini*
in Mexico City, D. F. (Tenochtitlán), Mexico
for purposes of Rallying all true Patriots and Lovers of Freedom in the ongoing Time
of Troubles and for Edifying the Young

Abeunt Studia in Mores

I. Apostrophe

Beloved country, unto you I render this witness, a beacon of hope in your ages-long

toil to rise out of Darkness, to carry forth the light of reason sparked by Montezuma,

raised by Cortés, fanned briefly by Iturbide, rescued by Hidalgo — a fragile candle that

once more flickers precariously in this hour of struggle against the base

encroachment of the Gaul; I salute you and relinquish to you my life, my tears, my

hot blood in service to that great day when all Men shall stand united whilst

tyranny, ignorance, the vile black vestiges of the past, shall all lie at last smoldering

and sputtering in cinders at their feet.

Time has blunted my memory in the intervening years since the events I shall

describe, yet Chronos could never vitiate the profound impression and lasting effect

that brief period produced upon my person — indeed upon the very core of my

aroused being. If I paint this beginning in somewhat melodramatic hues, it is solely

to render unto the reader some faint idea of the centrality of this narrative to my

life, of the immortal aspect taken in my recollection, stamped on my very soul, by

the incidents I shall forthwith record after two decades of silence. To them do I owe

no less than the entirety of my person: truly, they shaped me into what I am; they

were the forge that fired the raw mettle of a young man and transmortified him into the being that now inscribes these words across a chasm of years.

Indeed, across two chasms. For these events, burning and scintillating out of an already remote past — could indeed so much have altered so quickly, o my tragic nation? — shall cast warmth and light on a future even now taken root amongst the ruins of our own catastrophes, previous and actual. It is to those men striving today, tomorrow and forever to construct that blessed vision out of base clay, that I devote this missive. Be strong, you titans of virtue in this trying epoch, when our dreams and all that we have built stand shaken to their very foundations, both for us in the land of the star-gazing Aztec, snarling and clawing under the boot of an ersatz Bonaparte, and there, in that noble neighbor to the north, that torch of nations, cloven in two by that egregious conflict from which she shall emerge — I aver — stronger and more vigorous for having 'scaped the chrysalis of a backward, primordial past.

Finally, I consign these faint symbols, etched in parchment by the flicker of a dim taper in Mexico's darkest hour, to my own progeny. It is to you, my children, I bequeath this legacy, this history — it is so — this mnemonic heirloom of a life lived, a struggle served, a character molded in fire and sweat, an eternal quest embarked upon. For we sought nothing less than our future; yea, we sought it with faith, with hope, with reason and determination and the best intentions endowed us by Enlightened thought — and we found it, we found it. Read these words, my heirs, set down with love and expectation, and absorb to the profoundest depths of your strong hearts their lesson — and continue ever the struggle.

II. A Burgeoning Republic

The year 1839 found me, a budding medical student from the Capital, on a voyage of discovery in the vibrant young republic of Texas, itself freshly escaped from the orbit of Mexican tyranny and outworn rule. Far from sharing so many of my countrymen's enmity for the land so recently lost to us under the folly of the centralist dupe Santa Anna, I had ventured forth to see with my own eyes the noble precepts of republicanism enacted in the mediums of soil and flesh and industry. (This was, of course, in the days before that tragic affair sealed in '48 with the Treaty of Guadalupe-Hidalgo — truly the vilest document ever penned by man or Mammon. But I shan't dwell on the moral lapses of a vitally progressive state)

Like the venerated Sarmiento, I crossed the vale into the Protestant, prosperous north (that land that drew the envy of all Latin America to itself as a moth to the flame), seeking the keys to unlock my own country's entrenched benightedness. For the sun of democracy and brotherhood was dawning, then as now, in that fabulously rich territory, heaven-kissed; from its plateaus could one make out the very summit of that highest civilization envisioned by our forefathers in hallowed antiquity. Though only 24 years of age, and having contended at length with my father for permission to embark on my journey (my studies would have to yield temporarily to my zeal for glimpsing this fabled land of the future), already I saw in the raw wilderness of Texas — steadily being crafted and shaped by thousands of ardent democratic hands — a virgin nation, verily the model of nationhood, as had Sarmiento in his travels throughout the American East. As the Argentine saw civilization rising like a seismic force in iron and stone and industry, in the sublime man-made canyons of New York, so I beheld a new ethic of law, order, and brotherhood erecting itself in this vast region so long left to slumber in dumb chaos and disuse through a species of nescient imperial myopia.

This vast beehive of enterprise in the north was no accident.

In contrast to the fatuous anti-immigration Law of 1830 (my reader well knows), the new Texas republican government had opened the floodgates to settlers from the East, with land grants and enticements to all honest men who sought to build the inchoate nation out of the very earth itself. It was these aspiring, inspiring people I saw on my travels up through the former Nuevo Santander, following the old Camino Real; I saw them upraising their homes and plantations on the sites of the ancient *jacales,* carving districts and counties out of *departamentos,* rearing cattle and cotton to bolster a young economy under Houston's stewardship (when under Mexican rule so many resources had simply gone fallow). Now at last the riches of Texas were being tapped, and the land stirred, roused from Hypnos' oubliette, and spread proud new wings.

One blotch only, one lamentable blemish did my young eyes spy upon this pearl of democracy — and that was the hated mart of flesh Sarmiento had already noted as so paradoxical a feature of this young nation founded on the most egalitarian of ideals. For it was the scourge of human bondage, so I thought, that weighed the republic down even as it fueled its economy and bore Texas aloft into the community of nations. Those pathetic wretches I saw singing and sweating in backbreaking labor in the fields, or changing my horses at the post stations, their eyes vacant and dumb, their bodies thin and reeking of the mire, these were the unfortunate ones upon whose backs the proud new country emerging all around me won its prosperity. My reader, I am sure, needs no reminder that Mexico had long condemned the practice of slavery as incompatible with the *ne plus ultra* of human aspiration (it had indeed been a key issue in promoting the wedge between center and periphery, a wedge that grew to a canyon the width of the Rio Grande*. But enough of ancient history; unsettling as these visions of affliction may have been, it was to the future, not the past, that my coach conveyed me, and I seized that future with all the zeal and drive coursing through the veins of youth.

My father — after protracted battles and tears that need scarce interest those that peruse these lines — had agreed to let me interrupt my medical training for one year on the condition that I occupy myself productively in the north; the family's connections had therefore secured for me a post as foreign correspondent to the *Herald.* Settling in San Antonio de Béxar, the ancient capital of our former colony, I took up my duties with a zeal as bottomless as the azure Texas sky, an intensity to match that of the merciless Texas sun, and an assiduity that frankly astonished my perhaps more jaded colleagues at the bureau. I found the journalistic profession, while at times unsavory to the more delicate aspects of my station, nonetheless the perfect vehicle for exploring the young republic; my assignations — doubtless the choicest opportunities procured for me by my family's influence — led me up and down the territory to report on the elections, economic activity and human labors that form the very backbone of a thriving democracy.

Despite my rudimentary grasp of English — recently installed by the legislature as the official language of state (hardly an objectionable policy, given the influx of northerners) — I had little trouble maneuvering through the corridors of influence and decision, as I was always provided with interpreters or otherwise devoted my dispatches to the changing fortunes of the Mexican enclaves now outnumbered, but

----

* "Rio Bravo" in original, the Mexican name for the Rio Grande River for most of the 19th century (see pg. 13) — Translator's notes to be marked by asterisks.

still considerable, in the region. For my country was starved for news of its northern sister in those early days of periodical reportage, and it was my proud occupation to labor as one of a handful of those who met that need. (My longtime readers, of course, will be familiar with my Texas dispatches from this period; those who are not may access them at the Navarro family archives in Mexico City).

It is true, and I say this in passing, that I did on occasion sense a certain friction from our Anglo brothers, who saw in my olive skin and black eyes the image of the "vermin Tejano," whom many thought should be driven outright from the territory he had lorded over for centuries. Indeed, many were ousted, quite unceremoniously, even amongst the best families of Béxar society. I report this lamentable fact only to further set the stage for the drama I shall forthwith describe, and make plain my faith that these unwarranted prejudices shall wash out and fade away under the brilliant effulgence of the Lone Star, that Phoebus-like republic, so-longed for and so near at hand.

III. A Propitious Meeting

[Vásquez and Bell refer to each other throughout the text using the formal *usted* mode of address, while Castorito and the others are consistently addressed in the informal *tú*. — Trans.]

It was in San Antonio de Béxar that I first encountered the fascinating figure whom such a considerable portion of my narrative will concern. Through my sources I obtained an audience with a man who, it was said, shared many of my most fervent hopes for progress along the Enlightened model of reason adumbrated in the previous century — and moreover held both the determination and the means to forge those hopes into action.

The time was Fall, scarcely a month after Texas had attained, thanks to Count De Saligny's favorable report, its long-sought-after recognition as a legitimate state by a European power (indeed by the very cradle of revolutionary thought, despite that cradle's defilement by subsequent and ongoing disasters).

The man — never did that sobriquet fall on such deserved shoulders! — was to pass through the city on a scientific expedition, some sort of safari in quest of a fabulous indigenous creature. This was the information relayed to me by my peers at the bureau, normally rather aloof to me, it was true (due to my father's overbearing influence, I suspect), but in this instance quite forthcoming with a tidbit to what promised to be an intriguing story.

I soon learned all, and intriguing it undeniably proved to be. In the elegant lobby of the Hotel Borrego on West Commerce street, near the river, did I first strike up this beguiling figure's acquaintance. Well do I remember my first sight of him. Garbed in white, with a stylish cane and the quaint "cowboy hat" favored by so many in this virgin territory, a fiftyish man with white hair and a decidedly patrician mien emerged from the head of the red carpeted staircase that swept up before me, punctual to the minute of our agreed appointment, and fixed my gaze. Having taken the sum of my person at a glance, he briskly descended the steps and stretched out an arm, a smile contorting his ruddy face into a web of smooth wrinkles, and warmly greeted me in the most flawless, unaccented Spanish:

"Señor Vásquez, I presume? At your service. I am Captain Bell."

Immediately charmed by his manner, I met his hand in a friendly exchange and commented on his unusually elegant choice of cerements for a scientific outing to apprehend a wild creature.

"Ah," he smiled, explaining this away as one of only three vices he succumbed to in life: he considered it his prerogative as a gentleman to pack with him, wherever he went, and under whatever circumstances, a fine Benigni suit befitting his station. "A rather dandyish, Continental weakness, I admit." I did not point out the incongruity of the cowboy hat with such an outfit, but I had long observed, as had Sarmiento, that this new world sometimes eclectically, often capriciously, and for me always with the utmost naive and winning charm, rewrote the rules of the old as it saw fit. Given its mission, in my estimation, it had every right.

Cpt. Manfred Dodgson Bell, as he himself explained to me in the hotel's restaurant over a bottle of magnificent if costly '27 Amontillado — "My second vice, alas." — had studied the Biological sciences at the Sorbonne and once served the King of Belgium as liaison to the Ambassador to Spain (hence his mastery of that tongue). He would eventually relinquish his commission and make his fortune trading railway shares, helping to build the iron roads that linked the Continent. This accomplished, and seeking greener pastures, the Captain more than a decade previous had traversed the ocean to establish the Bell colony in the far north of the newly-opened territory of Texas. He came, enticed by land grants offered to Europeans by the Mexican imperial policy, at a time, as the reader will recall, when my country sought non-North Americans to populate the frontier as a bulwark against U.S. encroachment.

And yet this was indeed the sort of man the current Houston administration's immigration policies were designed to attract: refined, yet rugged and hard-working; experienced in matters of management and community organization, yet also bestowing fine European culture to the unsettled wastes of the frontier; practical, yet imbued with the great humanist principles, the nuances of rational and empirical thought, that drive great nations. Of German-Belgian parentage, commanding five languages, Bell had through charisma alone inspired a colony of 1,000 Bohemian, German and Austrian settlers to abandon their homes across the ocean, set foot on the wild and chancy shores of Texas, and strive to build, under his guidance and with the honest toil of their bare hands, a brave new world. Such carriage! Such grace! I had never met, in my callow youth, such an imposing, galvanizing figure. Before our first glasses were disembogued, I knew I had to somehow join his expedition, and forthwith inquired about the object of his latest scientific interest.

He hesitated a moment — his eyes darted over me again, as if unsure whether to take me into his confidence. Then he leaned forward in a conspiratorial gesture, stroking the white whiskers on his chin, and softly uttered:

"I seek ... El Gregín, señor."

I confessed ignorance of this animal, if such it was.

"Ah," he leaned back, filling his seat. "A wondrous creature. Exceedingly rare. Mammalian, the height nearly of two men. Nocturnal. Covered in black fur that shimmers like the Nile in the pallid rays of Dian's moon. I tell you in confidence, señor, that I have been quite obsessed with capturing one alive since the earliest days of my studies. It was then, in the library of the anthropology faculty, as an impressionable young man not much older than you are now, that I quite arbitrarily came across a description of the creature in a musty century-old text. It had been written by a certain Bolívar, a member of the Alarcón expedition. You will recall they trekked into this territory, later christened Tejas y Couahuila, to survey the King's holdings, as their counterparts Lewis & Clark did only decades later under Jefferson.

"Bolívar noted that El Gregín was worshipped as a deity by the Barankawa Indians in the South, though even they had never seen one up close or in any detail. The physical features I recounted to you just now nearly exhaust Bolívar's own description of the animal, as reported to him by the savages. You are also aware, I have no doubt, that this tribe, while once plentiful along la Bahía, is now quite extinct. Displaced from this world by progress, as it were. This unfortunately leaves us with no new means of obtaining direct visual testimony as to the habits or particularities of the creature. We are left only with rumors, fragments of myth.

"One of these indicates that El Gregín migrates south at this time of year — perhaps as far as the bosom of your own beloved country, señor. Its movements, haphazard and ever shielded by darkness, would bedevil the ablest tracker. The beast is notoriously shy of men. But I have a good suspicion that it will pass through the wilderness directly southwest of here, and on into the former Nuevo Santander, avoiding the trails and roads frequented by human travelers, in consequence of its ages-old migration routes having been disrupted by the recent wave of settlement in this region. If El Gregín still roams the *llano,* my dear señor Vásquez, it is my firm intention to ensnare it for science and display on my estate, thus to disprove the assertions of churlish learned men who dismiss this prodigy of nature as a mere savage's chimera. This is my third attempt at such a seizure, and as you can see I've not many serviceable years left me in which to try again. I should say that this is my last, best chance. Yet I am a man, if I may say so, unaccustomed to failure. Like you, I am a being motivated to positively get what he is after, even to the extent of leaving his home for the adverse conditions of the wild. I can confess to you that I chose to settle in what would become this new republic not only for the riches it promised, the challenge it represented, but to fulfill, albeit as an old man, the dream of a puerile, starry-eyed youth three decades gone. And so, if it is at all possible to apprehend this magnificent 'varmint,' as the Americans might say, this rapturous 'bugbear' as we Europeans would put it, then my military grounding, the record of my past coups, my very genealogy, so to speak, all make me more than confident of success."

Here he turned to me, fixed me with eyes of purest hazel.

"And I invite you, my young friend, to join us on this quest, either to report on our expedition for your paper as you see fit or to enlist in our little venture as, so to speak, a full-fledged member of our merry crew."

I ask my reader: how under God's Heaven could I possibly have replied in anything other than emphatic and eager affirmatives to the old man's offer?

IV. Into the Bush

The remainder of that evening was spent in addressing particulars of our journey, before retiring, at Bell's instigation, to a downtown performance by an Indian choir consisting of initiates of the Santa Beatrice Convent in nearby Goliad. I had no idea, firstly, that such indigenous musical troupes existed in this branch of the Texas wild — even in so cosmopolitan an island as Béxar — and second, that Indian voices could produce such dulcet, unearthly tones as those my ears apprehended that day. (Sadly, I've since learned this particular convent burned to the ground in 1852 under mysterious circumstances, its neophytes scattered to the winds. Anti-Indian sentiment was blamed.)

To my delight, the group of swarthy, wimpled women had deigned to discharge the divine Wolfgang's *Requiem*, a keen favorite — which I took as a decidedly beneficent omen on the eve of my excursion. Inwardly adrift in contemplation of this fortuitous journey, I was nearly startled out of my seat by the appropriately, if

unexpectedly, explosive opening to the *Dies irae,* delivered that night in a semi-
barbarous eldritch din:

> *Dies irae, dies illa*
> *Solvet saeclum in favilla:*
> *Teste David cum Sibylla.*
>
> *Quantus tremor est futurus,*
> *Quando judex est venturus,*
> *Cuncta stricte discussurus!*

The chorus clamored the prophetic verses such that my soul still reeled in odd
disquiet while I packed, posted my intentions to the editorship, and retired — in a
word, long after the fatal cacophony's final notes had ebbed.

Early the next day brought new companions: the two remaining members of our
expeditionary force.

The first, a disheveled and motley-dressed Indian, would serve as tracker. Called
Castorito, of the southern-ranging Libano Apaches, this squat, wiry figure with skin
of middle puce seemed always to keep low to the ground, as if perpetually ready to
escape a predator — or to pounce on prey. Enwrapped in his dark, downy *topolco*
(dubbed humorously by my people the *tápalo*)*, the man darted, rodent-like, from
pack to pack, readying our horses on the fringes of town where I joined the party,
and paid me little heed besides a gruff *"Buenos días."* He reeked of the bottle. Still,
his species' talents, not to mention his relative familiarity with the terrain south of
the hill country, would serve us in good stead. Moreover, and with no small
bemusement, I would soon discover this Indian's preternatural gift for the art of

----

* Vásquez's pun turns on the similarity of the Indian word to the Spanish for "cover it up."

sewing; his whole attire, from sturdy leather moccasins to double-stitched workshirt to incongruous bowler hat, was the fruit of his own industry. On our journey it seemed as if at every turn, be it by campfire or dawn's early light, I would spy the curious blade silently plying his craft.

The final member of our team was the youngest, a lanky tow-headed boy of some 16 years — the son of our good captain. William Charles Bell, a.k.a. Billy, certainly shared the solid build and penetrating gaze of his paternity. But it was with some alarm I noted, soon enough, that the youth, despite his blue blood, had gained little of the more delicate qualities from the fortune of his parentage. Where Bell was considered, Billy was headlong, perfervid and brash; where the father urbane, the son rustic, ill-mannered and blunt; where I saw in the captain only the finest distinction of man, in his charge I found merely a coarse, pockmarked whelp, a brazen bantling whose immediate disdain for myself I felt it a challenge not to answer in kind. To boot, the boy's prominent bucktooth, a decidedly unattractive feature that could only have come from the far side of his lineage, rendered his limited store of expressions irremediably stupid to my eye.

Shockingly, I soon learned it was the youth's ambition to grow rich as, of all things, a *baker*.

"Maybe make me 'nough jack to lead me an army, an' kick alla you darkies back 'cross the Nueces."

It was with difficulty that I managed to fathom the young braggart, his words thickly clogged with the accent of his region, but once I did, I had trouble deciding what was more insufferable: the brat's vulgar expression or his pitiable grasp of geography. His own revolution of '36 had established the border at the Rio Grande — though this frontier, true, would remain much in dispute for another decade.

"Pay him no mind," Bell counseled, visibly discomfited, when the boy had retreated. "As you can observe, señor, I have not been blessed with issue of ... Accept my apology for his manner. Billy has ever blazed his own trail, whatever my interventions. He can at times be ... difficult." (Here he forced a laugh.) "In sooth, I've often to tell him something thrice before he will do it, or regard it as true! But he is worthy, my friend. His courage is perfect, and this quality will serve us in good stead. You shall see."

And so we set off. Though hardly the crack team of scientists I had expected to ally myself with on this mission, our crew would more than function, I felt assured. Led by a man I respected implicitly, guided at its head by the Indian and the bitch Bela (a German shepherd specially reared to seek out our quarry's scent), and trailed by the boy, we soon crossed the tenuous rubicon dividing Béxar's outpost of civilization from the endless bush.

IV. A Bird

"Christ, sometimes it feels like we've been out here forever. An' it's all the same! Trees an' field an' cactus. Trees an' field an' cactus. Trees an' field an' cactus. Lordy, we could look us 'round this place forever an' never find a goddamned thing."

Such did the most artless among our party characterize the journey our third day out. Indeed, though we had found not our quarry, yet Billy's assessment proved lacking. There is a raw beauty to the southlands an eye more sophisticated than his will surely not ignore. Out past the hill country, which we'd long left behind, the land grows steadily flatter, the soil more parched and clay-like, though blanketed with vegetation: chiefly the oak, mesquite and common hedge brush, gradually joined by a species of palm as the north recedes. The harsh sun posed little trouble, as we restricted our movements, after the first day, to night, seeking El Gregín in its natural element. Unfortunately the moon was waning, making our passage through the thick chaparral (we avoided the established roads) a considerable nuisance. Often we were forced to dismount and guide our horses through the foliage, careful to avoid contact between our eyes and some stray branch. Gazing down once we'd reached a clearing, I saw my boots and trousers all but buried beneath a brindled carpet of burrs. Still, despite such constraints, we managed a good 20 miles a day through the difficult country in our relentless drive south.

We met hardly a soul on this journey; I remind my reader that at this time, in all of Texas (a territory roughly the dimensions of France) there resided, *in toto*, some 30,000 inhabitants, the vast majority to our north and east. We came only upon a tattered Indian village mired in the most appalling poverty and squalor I've yet witnessed; some Mexican sheepherders driving their stock up towards Corpus Christi (and who thought us rustlers until I served them my overtures of peace); and the occasional prairie wolf observing us hungrily from a distance. One of these Billy decided to take a shot at from his musket, prompting a heap of abuse from his father.

Bell grabbed the whelp by the hair and gave him a deserved yank. "Damn you, boy, you'll spook away everything within two miles! At times I think you've surely lost your head!" The boy would not resist him but with the fire in his eyes.

I made as if not to notice.

Of the humans we encountered, none reported seeing anything unusual. Castorito, who maintained a strange habit of looking askance when addressing his interlocutor, informed me he was doubtful of finding a usable or definite trail. The country was vast, Bela's nostrils cold.

"Not that I regret being on this ... trip," the Indian said one night, looking the opposite way. "I am an indigent wretch, Vásquez; you would very likely have found me in that miserable village of living dead we passed by were it not for the Captain. Aye, though not a literate man, I have learned more in his service than I could have gleaned from 70 volumes, surely."

My time with Bell all but confirmed such an opinion. My esteem for the man grew by the hour. Each night flew by as we discussed, in carefully whispered tones, every manner of subject; I found him adroit and even original on nearly all: the tumultuous and Byzantine history of Mexico since the Aztecs; the ethics of Berkeley; the burlesque and parodic twists in Cervantes. All the while he kept one eagle eye trained on the darkness, in reconnaissance for his prize, hiding somewhere in that vast dewy gloom.

If my estimation of the father increased with each exchange, my view of the son, tragically, only plummeted further with every attempt at rapprochement. The boy was something close to an idiot, certifiably so.

When I had first seen his pack mule, I asseverated that he'd grossly overloaded it with what were 42 items if they were ten; yet the boy would brook no criticism and accept no counsel, certainly not from me, to lighten the animal's load. The babe would have his toys. I subsequently noticed what we might term another odd detail: Billy was wearing several layers of clothing. One coat over another, one pair of trousers over another, and so on. Were it possible or convenient, I'm sure he would have worn seven coats and three pairs of boots all at once. When I asked for some light to be shed on the matter, he roughly told me only that he felt "win'er comin'." I shrugged and spurred my mount on.

The fourth day I spied a species of migratory bullfinch on the ground, its foot mangled by some predator it had escaped — or some buckshot it had only half-succeeded in dodging. Whilst it squawked and fluttered weakly in desultory fear, I sought to repair the terrified animal's limb. The others looked on. I cleaned, treated and dressed the wound with a bandage, which I figured would serve to protect the injury and speed it to convalescence. I then cobbled together a crude nest out of brittle sage grasses and twigs, and placed the bird in its makeshift home, out of predation's reach. I left with it a store of bread and water in a small beaker from my medicine bag, and we moved on.

Some hours later, sitting in a ring about the campfire while the east was just starting to blaze in majestic hues of orange and rose magenta, my companions questioned the night's quaint act of charity. Billy, in particular, seemed bewildered by such a show of good will to a creature he'd nearly been disposed to employ as target practice. He stared, his mouth dully agape in the fire's dance of light and shadow, while I explained my motives. Bell kept silent and listened.

"Kindness, the rendering of assistance and bestowal of proactive compassion, lad, is — or at the least should be — the highest aspiration of men and the hallmark of Christian love. (Castorito interpreted, sewing a new shirt.) I confess to a weakness, in particular, for the sufferings of animals. It is they, the noble and delicate denizens of the natural world, that most deserve our pity and succor."

"Wha' for?" the boy asked, befuddled.

I pondered how best to express this conviction in laymen's terms.

"Pain," I said, finally. "No pain is more purely felt, more terrifyingly experienced, than the pain of unreasoning beasts."

He was rather stumped by this assertion. I elaborated.

"Three years have I spent, Billy, studying the mysteries of the body at one of my country's finest medical colleges, the Bernal Institute in Guanajuato. In my slow initiation into the art of healing, I have been made privy to the myriad sites and sources and capacities of the human organism to suffer, to know intense pain. But it hardly requires a surgeon's learning to grasp that the vaster the jurisdiction of the nerves, the more fabulously complicated the mechanism — and no species can rival our own in this regard — the more vulnerable points are created, the greater the number of avenues for the ingress of pain. Yet as human beings, as the nonpareil ... that is, the highest example ... of our maker's craft, in our 'aspect so like a God,' as the bard said, we've always a doorway at hand to escape the mad flarings of pain."

"An' wha's that?" he asked.

I tapped, perhaps somewhat condescendingly, my own temple.

"Our brain, Billy. Our superior reason, whose seat resides here, in the armored chamber of our skulls. It is our rational capacities, our ability to leap beyond pain, to think it away, to rationalize it, interpret it, ultimately to absorb it into the fabric of our being for the benefit of a higher purpose, that in some sense grants us a blessed immunity from the tyrannical curse of pain."

The boy did not understand.

"Suppose, for a moment, using your imagination, if you please, that you have broken your leg ..."

"Broke my leg? How?"

" ... Perhaps in an accident. Your horse, for example, has thrown you ..."

"Uh-uh. She cain't. My Boots wouldn' never do that. I raised her right and she wouldn' never do that. Tell 'im, Castoreeto. My Boots wouldn' never .."

"I leave the cause entirely to your good imaginative powers. But however it has come about, envision in your mind's eye that you lie on a road, your leg fractured and causing you searing pain, 200 yards from where you know a medical station to lie. There you know to be bandages and a splint for your member, opium for your sufferings, water to soothe your parched throat. You need only traverse the distance and balm is yours. So you struggle, Billy, you move your body despite the agony burning in your shattered tibia, telling yourself: 'Only 100 yards more. Only 50 yards more. Only 20.' And so on. Even though you cannot see the shrine of your salvation — blocked as it is, perhaps by bush or leafage, or perhaps a ravine — you know it to be there. Perchance from having read it on a map, or having been informed of it by a colleague, you know — *without the benefit of actual perception* — that relief is near. So you move on, fighting the pain, telling yourself that soon, mercifully, it will all be over. You need only defer relief a few fleeting minutes, whilst you finish dragging yourself to release.

"Now, if you will ponder the issue a moment, my friend, I believe you will agree that an animal, a dumb beast of the wild to whose intellect your own, of course, is vastly superior, can do none of this. The animal has no sense of time, no knowledge beyond its limited instinctual birthright, no capacity to use its brain as a battering ram, to pierce the portcullis of pain. The animal knows only one thing: it suffers. As such, this pain expands to envelop its entire existence; all its body and brain are seized by it, gripped in its cold iron jaws, enslaved. Nothing is real for that poor creature except its pain; no knowledge of release, no rationalization of its horrified, suffering state can ease it from the agony that bursts every dam in its organism, that grows to encompass all its senses apprehend: an ontology of anguish. No hope, Billy. For the animal there is no escape. As such, despite their much more limited capacities and lower post on the ladder of life — indeed because of these shortcomings — the beast of the field knows a far greater spectrum of the pangs of undiluted suffering than man, armed with the sturdy hoplite buckler of his brain, can even imagine. Hopelessness, Billy, the nadir of affect, is the zenith of torment. And it is this very despair, through its inaptitude to hope, that an animal experiences exclusively when condemned to its prison of pain."

The boy did not answer. I believe he may have been drowsing off. The pools of his eyesockets, opaque as pitch in the weakening embers' light, yielded little clue to his expression — if indeed he had any. We sat in silence. But after a few seconds, spent observing the fire, hearing its final crackles and sputters, Castorito deftly applying his needle, Bell adjusted his position on the turf and addressed me.

"And what, my dear Vásquez, do you regard as the primary component, the *sine qua non*, of pain?"

I pondered. "Paracelsus, señor, I believe, defined it in mnemonic terms. Pain is memory. The memory of fear, which, I have sought to prove, for animals is quite acute in contradistinction to our own."

"Indeed. And I ask you, señor, fear of what?"

"Why, fear of death. Pain is the memory, branded on our very souls, of that earliest epoch when our ancestors were driven from Eden, when first we knew the reaper. It is the physical acknowledgement of that ineluctable fiend we humans so often choose to disremember, whose merest touch makes dust of dreams, that laughs to scorn our fiercest and most tearful disavowals. Pain and fear, señor, are of a piece, two sides of a coin honored by that banker with whom it is the destiny of us all to one day have exchange."

"I see, my friend," he replied, a tired smile forming on his lips. "Beholding the weakest and most pitiable of God's creations overwhelmed by a proxy of the most powerful, undeniable force — a proxy we as the maker's chosen species can hold at bay through our intellect — you seek to intervene, in your own modest fashion. To bring some temporary comfort to those least equipped to face the unfaceable."

We regarded each other's illumined aspects across the dancing tips of the flames, our silhouettes in stark relief against the diluting murk.

"You have fixed me as ever, señor. I confess I cannot tolerate to gaze upon a creature, whatever its aspect or form, while it suffers. I cannot countenance the very thought. It is itself painful, alien, an outrage to my own mayhap too delicate sensibilities."

Once more, as had happened more than once during our journey, I saw that light enter Captain Bell's eyes: the light of a soul buoyed by the proximity of true kinship.

"My dear lad," he uttered. "I am touched more than I can phrase in words to encounter such unalloyed nobility — and in this wilderness, of all locales! You are Candide, you are Tristan, your heart is pure and uncorrupted. Keep it ever so, my young friend."

We both wallowed in that warm flush of sentiment, of intimate connection, that comes solely from congress with a fellow traveler — though its effect was somewhat muted by the intrusion of the boy's sudden and explosive snores. He slept, loudly, salivating against Castorito's arm. Bell therewith declared a rest and we wordlessly retired.

VI. A Southern Belle

We were riding, near the sunrise of our sixth day, when I experienced one of the oddest sensual quiddities of the prairie. We proceeded along as normal, gazing in all directions along the flat expanse, far and wide, for our prey. In an instant the wind visibly, tactilely, arose from slumber. Within a scant minute, the temperature must have dropped some 12 degrees. My thermometer, held up to the air, confirmed this. It was as if some huge doorway to a vast subterranean cavern had split open at our backs, admitting the chill of the netherworld. A Norther, the Texians call it. Billy, who had proven a prophet, gloated not in his work of Cassandra, but rather fetched another layer of clothing from his pack and covered himself further, breathing not a word.

We fortunately did not long remain in this inclement cold. Castorito rode back to us, the dog bolting excitedly at his side, to report the nearness of a small cotton plantation, a mere three miles off. The Captain, reckoning our somewhat bedraggled company might profit from shelter and society after nearly a week in the bush, willed us thence.

But that was not all Castorito found. On our way to the plantation, he bade us stop to examine a patch of wooded ground that roused Bela's interest. Kneeling over this area, at the perimeter of an arid forest, we observed with mounting curiosity what resembled a track of some sort. There were toe marks, the vestige of a heel thrust a good two inches in the crumbly earth — yet both of an animal I had never before encountered. If anything, I would have said that the mark resembled the footprint of an elephant or other pachyderm, only more hourglass-shaped and considerably smaller. There were also some black splotches left in the area that I concluded to be fecal matter — watery and insubstantial, yet in a copious amount. Only one track did we find, indicating that either the creature could fly, stuck to the trees as its wont, or had simply left no other impression amid the densely vegetated turf overrun by the yucca. Bela whined and tossed her head, uncertain of a scent; the track was not fresh. After careful examination of the surrounding plants, however, Castorito felt confident the trail led deeper into the bush and not away from it — in a southerly direction.

After deliberating the matter while fingering his hat (a considerably more battered model than the one in which I'd met him), Bell decided against immediate pursuit, given that the sun would soon break and the quarry was likely far from here. To my own suggestion that we take heart from our first physical sign of the creature's presence in this region and press on, he rejoined that he felt positively certain seeking El Gregín by day would only tire our party further, to no good end.

And so we moved on to the property of a Mrs. Annabelle Lytton. We learned our hostess' name soon after inquiring at the gate for a meal and a few hour's repose. The porter, an ancient white-haired slave, though somewhat startled by our unannounced appearance (which had moved him from sleep), soon brought back word that his mistress, satisfied we did not comprise a Comanche raiding party, bid us enter.

The plantation's central two-story house, though somewhat dilapidated, resembled many of the sort scattered throughout the hinterlands, the legacy of farmers and cattle raisers whose forebears had received land grants from the Spanish crown or subsequent governments. Set off some distance from the fence, this central area of barns and stables was where we dismounted in anticipation of welcome. It was rather long in coming.

The occasional slave darted hither and thither, looking us over quickly before averting his gaze and proceeding on his errand. An institution such as this would own perhaps 30 or 40 of his caste. We heard shouts and angry calls from somewhere behind the building. It proved indeed awkward, albeit seemingly unavoidable, to stand before the entrance some ten minutes, while the place blossomed into activity with the rising sun. Obviously our arrival had imposed upon their usual routine, I thought.

Dawn had long broken ere a trio of our party was led inside at last by a dusty, sun-weathered Anglo in a brown work hat, who apologized for the egregious delay. His accent thicker than Billy's, I was hard-pressed to catch his words.

Soon enough the captain, Billy and I were seated at table, the Indian barred from setting foot indoors. He'd seemed accustomed to the practice.

Mrs. Lytton, a widow from Biloxi, soon appeared, and with her (I hoped) that particular brand of good cheer and uplift only the company of the fairer sex can bestow.

Yet I feel compelled to confess to my reader that, despite my initial delight at being cast once more upon an isle of the civilized world, the ensuing exchange soon degenerated this elation at my good fortune into its very opposite.

The woman, despite radiating what passes in this republic for "Southern charm," alarmed me with her boorish opinions and atrocious asseverations on the question of slavery. Almost immediately upon greeting us and seating her ample frame (they did not receive many guests, we were told), this portly "reformed abolitionist," as she described herself, launched full-tilt into a stream of complaints about her "saucy" bondmen. Bell translated for me, though I could have done quite without hearing such outrageous idiocies.

"Yes, I'd just as lief whip a slave as not," Mrs. Lytton said, over a spread of eggs and ham she duly devoured. "There exists no other recourse. Let the other week serve as my example. I told Baby, I told her, 'Take those new piglets out of the big pen, put 'em with their momma over in the smaller stall.' I told her and told her, gentlemen, assuredly, 'Keep 'em away from that big bull, he'll stomp 'em, Baby, he will. Baby, you better do it,' I told her, 'You better do it.' But wouldn't you know? Wouldn't you know? She leaves the piglets right in the pen, and right the next mornin' I finds 'em all squashed and half-chomped and all stomped to shit!"

(She was given to such wild and vertiginous contrasts in her choice of expression — the sign of an unfocused mind.)

"$100, sir, $100 those pigs could have fetched me at the Béxar market when grown. $100. Why, you're so dumb, Baby, I tell her, you're so dumb you'd buy hail insurance in summer."

And here she let out one of her characteristic shrieks. I clenched my fist about the fork.

Surely, I asked the woman, her former country's history of subjugation (she was Irish) had sensitized her to the plight of other downtrodden folk? Was it not once her belief that the slave was worthy of admission to the league of freedom?

"It was, sir. Indeed. In Ireland, as a babe, I had every intention of upholding the rights of their race, yet two years here and already I've learned that the only right they deserve is the right to frequent whippings, aye, and most assiduously performed! It's the only language they understand. You saw what an effort it took my man Brick to get your bags unloaded, your horses taken away and stabled. Why, he had to yell, threaten to box their ears like children, before they'd move their lazy carcasses and do as they was told. This sauciness is typical. Typical. Typical. A nightmare, gentlemen, simply a nightmare to run a plantation in this manner. And yet without our stock of slaves, we could of course never afford to plant our cotton, let alone pick and process it. But they're saucy. Saucy. I had to have one killed last year, for tryin' to stick Brick with a knife. Can you believe? Out here in the boondocks, we've got enough troubles just survivin' between the Indians and the droughts and the god-damned Mexicans! Me, I've seen the error of my ways. By all means, gentlemen, leave the slave in his place, I say, and spur him on to his duty by all means, all means. If a few eggs get broke along the way, well ... that should only serve as a right lesson to the rest of the basket!"

And again she produced a high-pitched cackle at her own "witticism."

Not that some of the widow's anxieties were without foundation. We need not remind the reader of that era not so very long ago, when the frontier languished, positively roiled, in savagery, an angry wasp's nest of murder, pillage and dissension, where the worst elements of the Old and New worlds plied their black arts unfettered by law. A mere generation can hardly serve to stifle the memory of that time when the waves of rampant criminality (receding, true, but by no means spent) surged and battered against the rocks of encroaching civilization.

A witch's brew of rumors constantly bubbled, pointing to plots between Mexico (livid at the loss of her former territory) and agitating Northern slaves. There had been several insurrections, escapes, violently suppressed; remember only the more than 60 lynched along the Brazos in '35, in the hysteria leading up to the war for independence. As for the more concrete anti-Mexican/Tejano sentiment, I have already alluded to its virulent manifestations throughout the land. It stung every fiber of my being, I readily admit, that this woman, who saw in my person merely a filthy "bandido," barely tolerated me at her table — and solely at Bell's insistence.

"This Córdova affair last year. What of that?" Mrs. Lytton continued, spitting slivers of ham onto her plate. "And this horrid Chief Bowles business!* These coloreds are always at the ready to unite in their mongrel armies, sir, to strike down their masters and reclaim this whole land for their filthy brood! These Mexes, they shoulda been slaves too! They shoulda, shoulda, shoulda!"

I reminded her, my throat taut, of the 60 Tejanos who gave their lives at the Alamo and San Jacinto, to fend off Santa Anna's mercenary troops — defending her right to sit at table in her bonnet and lavishly butter her biscuit to her heart's content. If the price of inclusion in this great young republic was to be paid with blood, my people had met that price in spades.

"Moreover, madam," I intoned with growing rage, "my countrymen are slaves to nothing but historical misfortune. Our constitution is modeled on your very own and that of other enlightened powers. As for the Córdova affair and those like it: fanatics, sadly, tread the soil of all nations. Let me assure you that the majority of my compatriots mean this state no harm. Mexico, lamentably, has far too many internal troubles at the moment to involve herself in international escapades. This entire territory lies now in your hands, and rightly so; believe me when I say we wish you well with it."

It was as if she had not heard me.

"This land's been claimed for Christ. The Protestant Christ. Never again shall it fall to the backward peoples of the South, nor to the inhuman hordes of Indians, and never, while we breathe, to the miscegenating Catholic, who peoples his heathen territories with freaks of nature, with monsters mixed with incompatible blood.

----

* Lytton refers to two of the most notorious Texas uprisings of the late 1830s.

The issue of your Spaniard, a second-rate European, mingling his seed with the Indian, its own blood of an order nearly as low as that of the African, why sir, the very thought of such a people repulses me! Repulses me unto sickness!"

I bolted to my feet; the chair's screech startled the butler.

"Madam, I can endure no more. This Catholic mongrel thanks you for breakfast and wishes you a good day."

And I stormed out.

I heard her shrieking laughter resounding through the hallway as I found my way out, expecting Bell at any moment to join me. He remained behind. Billy, for his part, had concentrated throughout on noisily downing his meal, on occasion nodding dumbly at the widow's statements.

The harridan's hideous hypocrisy, her unreflective hatred and prejudice, were an outrage to my honor. But what riled perhaps most of all was that during our talk that infernal woman had cornered me into admitting my own shameful distaste for the race of the slave. But those simpering manners, crude childishness of demeanor, barren intellect and coarseness of frame, all of these surely were not inborn traits, but symptoms of the unendurable and lifelong torment of an inhuman system. This was not inferiority, but victimization! So thought I: the slave was neither inherently evil nor untrustworthy nor dumb; surely to remove the cause of his affliction meant to clear his path to full-fledged and actual humanity.

All this had fallen on fat, deaf ears.

I need not describe to my reader the humiliation I felt at being housed in a barn, at being compelled to make a bed of a stable with Castorito and the cur, while Bell and his idiot son reposed within the house. At one of my family's dinners in our capital, this woman would have been banished from the table as the uncouth and offensive lout she was, yet here it was she who forbade me her trust and friendship due solely to my lineage. Everything about her revolted me *in extemis*. I swore, grumblingly, covering myself with a coarse blanket that reeked of some animal's excretions, that I would never so compromise my character as to duplicate, even slightly, her vile retrograde model. So I believed: such vulgar specimens of humanity represented a mere stage (I brooded in silence), the base material from which a great nation was steadily emerging. Of this I was certain ...

Suddenly the Indian's voice, dulled by liquor, importuned upon my thoughts.

"What's the matter, señor? Could it be that your three years of study in the best university of México could not suffice to wash away your brown skin? And so you must lodge with us, here in this fine democracy of swine and barn rats? *Qué lástima, señor.* A pity, such a pity."

His laughter, like a babbling hyena's, tapered off in burbles of spume. I gnashed my teeth and said nothing, but despite my exhaustion sleep was long in coming to me that day.

VII. The Rancho

Late in the evening three days hence, mercifully far from the widow Lytton's revolting bulk, our fortunes turned.

Chasing the trail we emerged from a low forest of mesquite and bramble, choked by the ubiquitous chaparral, onto a grassy clearing — and onto another stage of the nigh endless flatland, cracked and parched but by no means unvegetated, leading south to the nearing frontier.

Castorito spotted a spike of fume in the distance, and Bell commanded to seek its cause. It lay in our direction, and a feeling of sudden unease inexplicably began to build within the party with every footfall of our approach. A half hour's journey through the persistent, stiffening cold brought us to the fire's source; our dread was confirmed. The scene that greeted us upon our arrival, punctuated by Bela's frantic barks and howls, rivaled the Biblical in rank horror.

We came upon a typical rancho, of the sort peppered throughout the Texas outback, run by humble and honest laborers of the land. Yet seemingly in an instant, through some malefic preternatural agency, the site had been transported to a corner of blackest hell. Its main cabin sputtered acrid smoke and flames from shattered windows. Household implements, farmers' tools , a child's doll, lay scattered about the ground. The corral had been opened and a small herd of cattle set free — not stolen; they ambled about, aimless, in the prairie, munching grass without a care, before the grisly unfolding spectacle. We immediately deduced that this pillage could not be the work of the thieving Comanches.

The first victim we found sprawled near the *jacal*. A Tejana in a blood-spattered skirt of plain Indian design, she yet flailed weakly, steeped in her own gore, coughing away the last moments left to her on this earth. Her wounds, I could see as I knelt before the woman, were irredeemably mortal.

Her bulging black eyes, upon seeing me, screamed an unspeakable tale that corroborated the state of her obliterated body.

"My God, Vásquez," Bell's voice came to me from somewhere above, "can you help her?"

"No," was my curt reply. I took not my eyes from her ruined form. "I can only ease her passage to the next world. Castorito, quickly, your bottle."

The knave was loath to part with his beloved Mescal, a small supply of which I knew he always carried in his coat pocket.

"Quickly, damn you!"

Tearing it from his grasp, I placed some drops upon the woman's lips and sought — in vain, I knew — to staunch the flow of blood from her jugular and abdomen. They had been ripped apart by fangs, claws — I knew not what. One other thing I noted, but the thought of it so repulsed me that almost as quickly I absented it from my mind. Her pulse already grew frightfully low. Bell addressed the woman.

"Se ... señora. Who, what did this to you? Was it El Gregín? Tell us, señora, please. El Gregín? We seek El Gregín. Was it El Gregín? El Gregín?"

"El ... el Gregín," she confirmed, almost in a whisper, her eyes slowly starting to roll up into her head. If ever she considered us more than phantoms, we had now utterly ceased to exist for her. Then, startlingly, she convulsed in her death throes, sought to sit up, and screamed with steadily rising volume in a voice no longer human:

"El Gregín! El Gregín! *El Gregiiiiiiiiiiiiiín!"*

The unholy sound perished on her lips as her body relaxed in its final sleep. Never had I witnessed such an appalling sight. The tears welled in my eyes. I had not even had time to administer laudanum from my medicine bag, to ease the suffering from her gashes. She had expired before I could prepare the proper dose.

I leaned forward, shut her lids forever. Still kneeling, I felt Bell's hand on my shoulder, reassuring, strong. She was the first person I had ever seen in my few years complete the return journey to our Creator. And in such a paroxysm of violence! I was seized with a thousand emotions, chief of which sorrow for this innocent creature I had never, could never have, known. But the day's horrors were hardly ended.

Billy ran back toward us from behind a small storage barn. He'd found another body. Castorito asked for his bottle back — I unceremoniously tossed it at his feet, from whence he greedily recouped it. We rushed to where the boy directed us. I noticed Bell, hard-pressed to keep up on his cane, had unsheathed his revolver.

The corse lay contorted on the ground, in a pool of blood. A man. Texian. Dead perhaps an hour. From the cadaver's neck protruded naught but a black rictus of torn flesh and tendon, a gush of coagulation spread out before it in the pattern obtained when a large bucket is flushed out all at once. The man's blond head lay several feet away, face turned away from the purpling sky. There was evidence of struggle: dragged tracks, scuffed boots, the hands in fists. The wind began to pick up, lolling eerily on the plain, catching and dispersing our clouds of breath almost as quickly as they flew from our lips. The soles of our boots, meanwhile, were already encrusted with fast-drying blood; in the rush of events and stimuli, it seemed we wallowed in a veritable bog of it. My heart thundered.

Bell commanded Billy and Castorito to take the dog and quickly seek a trail; this destruction was quite recent. As the boy and the Indian shuffled away, the wind shifted, bearing an odd smell to our nostrils. It somewhat blended with the smoky odor emanating from the cabin, but carried its own dreadful stench of char. We sought the source. We found it, hanging by the branch of a nearby tree. I had peripherally noticed this dark, swaying lump in the confusion of events up to that point, though my near-sightededness had precluded any immediate identification. I had absently presumed it a bee-hive or bird house of some sort. It was not. Upon approach, the still lightly-smoking object resolved itself into — it is difficult to describe it.

Swinging in the wind from a thin chain, approximately at the height of my chest, mottled with the colors of burnt coal and honeydew pulp — this was the image that came to me — we found an infant, perhaps two years old, hanged and consigned to fire.

I grew quite senseless at that point. The accumulated shocks had finally conspired to relieve my stomach of its contents, while Bell could only stand there, stolid. He at length offered me his handkerchief. Poking his cane into the ground, he coaxed light clouds of dust that caught in the wind. It was now deepest twilight. I recovered more swiftly than I would have thought, my stomach emptied. I drank from my canteen, mulled over, grasped for, ultimately failed to find the words to address a spectacle that transcends language. Yet still I had to speak.

"Captain," I said, my voice raw. "The time has come for you to tell me precisely what manner of creature we are pursuing. I demand to know. I believe you have been less than completely open with me about the nature of this beast."

He kept inspecting the soil with his faux scepter. I continued.

"That man was decapitated, probably with a machete, I should venture to guess. This poor child had its neck placed in a noose, its entire body set aflame, by intelligent hands. And that woman. Captain, that woman was violated. Carnally. Her gashes were inflicted through bites, clawings, from a being of prodigious strength and admired viciousness. Yet the trauma marks and footprints are inconsistent with a creature of El Gregín's stature, as you described it to me."

"That I was not aware of," he quickly retorted. "In all the Barankawa legends, the creature's height is reported as twice that of a man."

"You admit, then, to knowing more than you told me?"

He bowed his head, returned to his cane's insistent jabs, whose reverberations I felt through my boots on the splotched and bruise-colored ground beneath me.

"Yes, my friend. Not very much, mind you. But this sad scene we have come upon does confirm certain ... rumored aspects of the animal's behavior."

"So this Gregín is not so benign and 'shy' a creature as I was led to believe."

"I said only that it would avoid human contact as its first, essential course. But you can see that the incursion of settlers throughout this region makes this less and less ..."

"Forgive me, Captain, but I cannot credit you. Why would this creature come here and willfully attack peaceful farmers? I can understand such an atrocity from brutish savages like the Comanches, but this animal's primary, inborn drive — especially if aware of our pursuit — would be to continue its migration south at all cost. No creature of instinct would ..."

"I never said, my friend, that it operated solely on instinct."

These words unsettled me more than I can aver. I felt almost as if trapped, as if suddenly finding myself on a vessel plying unknown waters in a nameless void.

"What do you mean by that, señor?" The question left my lips a whisper.

He sighed. The subsequent explanation offered sufficed to chill me to my bones, not only for its content, but for the curiously detached manner in which this man I so admired suddenly assumed to deliver it.

"They were mere legends, my friend. Stories from a dead, primitive culture. I scarcely gave them a thought. I'm not sure that I do even now, despite what would seem overwhelming evidence. But Bolívar's account does infer that the savages took El Gregín for a god not only for its wondrous shape and enigmatic mystique, but because they feared it utterly to the depths of their ignorant souls. I told you no one had actually seen a Gregín up close. That was not entirely accurate. There were a number of unfortunate beings, the Barankawa reported, who had gazed full upon the face of El Gregín — and none survived the event. For it is part and parcel of the legend, my friend, that he who actually sees El Gregín is doomed to pay with his life, in the most horrifying manner, for the privilege; that all who gaze upon the monster shall vanish utterly from the face of the earth and never be seen by living eyes again."

The howling wind roused itself further. Venus emerged in the night sky, shining weakly through thickening mist. A cold sweat trickled along my back.

"Worry not, lad," Bell concluded, took me by the arm, led me back towards the main house. "It hardly befits our station as men of reason to be swayed by such, what do the Americans call them? 'Tall tales'? All this is merely the benighted superstition of an extinct people too unsuited, too ill-equipped and retrograde, to remain in this world. We are the living, Juan. They perished because they could not embrace progress. But men as we are the thinkers of our age. Our mission, I know you agree with me, is to pierce the veil of darkness, to defuse the false traps set before us by pitiable regressives and to expose the truth through rigorous rational inquiry. Be bold, my comrade. We have embarked on a glorious venture, a true scientific quest. Reason our torch, discovery our destination. These poor souls, lamentably, have been lost — but not in vain. Like the sacrificial victims of your Aztec ancestors, Juan, whose blood was spilled and spirits delivered unto the sun god that he might batter back the forces of night, these people's flesh has been transmuted by providence itself into the fuel that keeps Reason — our own Quetzalcoatl — aflame!; their lives were small, you'll agree, but through their deaths they have cast a blazing, brilliant spotlight onto our path and shown us proof

— clear as day, is it not? — that our quarry does, undeniably, roam this earth. This alone we should retain as a spur to our mission. You are with me, Juan, are you not? I can count on your cooperation in this venture — to the end?"

I only nodded, grimly. But internally I wavered as I grew to suspect, with mounting dread, that the Captain's mind itself was wavering — between sanity and its farthest bourne. For how else to countenance this fit, this glory-seeking vanity at the risk, nay, the very real holocaust, of innocents? I stopped, stood firm. He turned to me.

"Captain Bell, if this creature is capable of such carnage, our course is clear. We must ride back to Béxar, or at least the nearest large settlement, and alert the local militia."

His visage darkened.

"No, my friend. For several reasons. Firstly, we would lose at least half a day in doubling back as you suggest. Second, these rural militias are crude, undisciplined rabbles of peasants. We've had dealings on past expeditions with their kind. Provided they could even get here within a day — a doubtful prospect — they would find the animal's trail long cold. Barring that, if they actually succeeded in finding the creature — can you imagine what damage they might cause our prize? These are ersatz minutemen, used to fending off Comanches and brigands indiscriminately with old muskets. No. El Gregín requires a far lighter touch — a scalpel, my dear healer, not a hatchet. We are here, we are closest to our quarry. We know with what we are dealing. As scientists, we are best suited to apprehend the animal with negligible harm."

"Captain, you unilaterally assume responsibility for these men's lives, and mine as well. That is, under the present circumstances — forgive me — an impetuous, dictatorial act."

He steeled, held his cane firmly in both hands.

"Vásquez, I am a military man, accustomed to such burdens. I am likewise in the habit of seeing my orders obeyed. Moreover, and to the point, I am categorically determined to capture my quarry alive. It is worthless ... it is of no use to me, to science, dead." Suddenly he softened again. "But I cannot stop you, of course. If you choose to detach yourself from us and return to civilization, you will find none of our party barring your way." Here he smiled, stepped forward, pressed my arm. "And you've quite a story for your dispatches already, eh?"

While I mulled this, we returned to the smoldering farm house, where Billy and Castorito met us coming back. They sweated despite the cold.

"The wind dissolves the trail, Captain. Bela is confused, though I believe we have enough to track. It's run off to the South, back into the brush. It could not have gotten far."

"She's got 'im, Paw. She's got a good scent. But the bastard's got a good hour on us, an' in the woods, now it's dark, it'll be harder to track the sumbitch."

"We'll refrain from such tags for it, Billy. We could, after all, be dealing with a *female* Gregín."

"Yes, sir."

"One other thing, Captain," the Indian said, looking out towards the last glimmers of the sun's glow. "There's a storm coming. From the northwest. A big one. It will be here by this time tomorrow."

I decided to remain with the party; Bell's arguments (quite sane, upon reflection) having dovetailed with my own professional ambitions. Yet I insisted we take the necessary time, the object of our chase being so close, to bury the dead. This we did, in three hastily prepared plots crowned by crude wooden crosses. The anonymous infant's blasted face, black and heart-rending as I poured hallowed earth over it, was a sight that shall haunt me to the end of my days. I vowed then that I would somehow, for the love of God, whatever the cost to my body and soul, atone for my failure to bring succor to these innocent, ruined lives.

In pace requiescat!

VIII. The Storm

There was a change in the mood of our company as marked as the severe turn of weather. The latter inspired us with awe at the Proteus-like climes on the open grassland; the former, fueled by the destruction we'd witnessed, filled us with reluctance and dread for our fate.

Even more swiftly than the Norther had descended upon us days before, the storm rushed up at our backs like a hungry predator, eager to devour us into its maw; the hunters turned prey. It fell just as Castorito had predicted, late the following evening — ruining our chance at sleep after an enervatingly full day of forced march at the Captain's insistence, in pursuit of our nearby quarry.

The suddenly starless, blackened sky was split first by the howl of wind, which slammed into us with gale force and little warning — Bell's hat flew — then was positively rent asunder by lightning, an unholy flash that for a millisecond illumined the vastness of the plain brighter than a thousand suns. Then came the thunderclap, an assault on the senses that, for all my scientific learning, catapulted me to paroxysms of alarm on par with the most benighted Medieval ignoramus. Then, out of the shattered eggshell Heavens, the rain ...

But I see again my pen falters. Words scribbled by a quivering old man's hand

are puny things, limpid and bootless, against the majesty and fury of that tempest

which turned all our world, all our senses and thoughts, to water. We were caught

helpless as mice on the plains. We had little choice, in our exhaustion, but to press

on to a small cluster of trees in the distance, itself battered and blowing in the wind,

and try as best we could to shelter ourselves and our stores from the endless celestial

pelting. Very soon we were the picture of misery.

But not all; one among us succumbed not to woe, to the battering storm, to our

isolated circumstances in the wilderness south of the Nueces.* This lone exception

was Bell: he never seemed more alive, more intent, more manic, more a rock of

determination and ardor, than now, when he sensed his prized object so near

within his grasp — tempest be damned.   A white haired Lear, he boomed his

challenge to the Heavens, one gnarled fist in the air, and again I feared for his sanity.

But we had still other troubles mounting. It was a struggle to calm our horses in

the merciless gale, even under the crude shelter of mesquite, while rest became but

the cruel joke of an unmoved God. Meanwhile, one of our party, the least and most

vulnerable, had already fallen victim to our quarry's preternatural cunning.

Scarcely two miles from the rancho (our hands still stained with the earth of

innocents' graves and as we galloped in hot pursuit of a promisingly fresh trail), an

agonized bellow burst from a clump of trees ahead, dark and mysterious in the

twilight. Traversing the thick shrubbery, we came upon Bela, enraged and whining,

snorting and foaming, literally bouncing off the trees in agitation.

An inspection showed she had sniffed two nostrils-full of some acidic, noxious

----

* The last major river before the Rio Grande and Mexico.

powder — I identified it as possibly a mixture of ground chipotle, perhaps purloined from the woman's stores at the rancho. It had quite unmistakably been left directly on the trail, a harmless-seeming clump, awaiting ingestion by our scent-driven guide. A trap.

"We must add a subtle deviousness to the catalog of this creature's endowments," I told the wide-eyed Captain. "As well as a keen intelligence."

"Now I'm certain," Bell replied. "It knows we are chasing it. We have our prey desperate, on the run. Now is the time to redouble our pace!"

And he would brook no delay, driving his troops three hours past their appointed rest time, and, when the prey still proved elusive — it had every advantage in this Stygian wood, the Indian said — acquiescing to only three hours respite before our forced march the following day.

One thing only gave me reason for hope: the strangely grooved and inconsistent tracks we regularly discovered, made as if by a heavy shuffling motion in the earth, along with the characteristic deposits of liquid sludge. This creature must be half-water, I mused. But there was a simpler explanation.

"Captain," I told him, "the animal may be quite ill. This fecal waste is consistent with the symptoms of cholera, a blight, as you know, that has bedeviled this region in recent years. If this is indeed a diarrhetic flow, the creature we are chasing might not survive the week."

He nodded grimly.

Despite the pain of her ruined nasal passages, our four-legged consoeur refused any ministrations on my part. I'd made the mistake of seeking to attend to her, apply some salve to her burn mere moments after the critical whiff — and narrowly escaped a mauling.

Now, several hours into the deluge that abated not its violence, I was the first to notice my would-be patient missing. I roused the others, but hoots and calls only confirmed that Bela had mysteriously slipped out of this surreal fever dream of exhaustion and dread that our world had become. This was hardly the time, and we were hardly in a state, to seek her out effectively. And so with the lassitude of fatigue, we conceded her departure to the fates.

Bela was gone.

IX. The Butcher

We pushed on at dawn's gray light, near-zombies, the four horsemen of apoplexy, with only our zealous Ahab to drive us on. The rain still fell heavily in the morn, though now in a more vertical path, and over the course of the day steadily tapered off to nothing. The storm had gone as quickly as it had arrived, in its wake leaving a universe of mire that made every step a double strain, and a galaxy of young streams we forded only with draining care and difficulty. Despite the excitement of — we still felt — a nearing resolution, we were all quite fagged. The lack of sleep and constant need to remain alert, on the lookout for a creature intent on eluding us, had worn us quite.   The horses, too, were close to their end. But suddenly, just after sunset on the second day of another forced movement, we were startled by a sudden shout.

"Just the spot!" Bell declaimed, licking his lip. "Just the spot for our quarry. I can taste it, I tell you!"

We all stood, rather mystified at the Captain's statement. We had come to yet another patch of the chaparral, quite thick now as we approached a gorged creek with its many streams and tributaries. There was nothing visible to distinguish this portion of the wilderness from the scores of miles we had already covered.

"We'll set up camp here," he insisted. "It's quite early yet. Then we shall spread out in circles of reconnaissance. He's near, I tell you, quite near!"

A shudder ran over my back, as when a man lost in the desert looks down to see his map gone utterly blank.

There was an abrupt thump, like a sack of potatoes dropped in the mud. Billy lay in a heap at the base of his mount, quite senseless. At first I ascribed this to the prostration we all shared, but a cursory glance at his pallid visage showed something more sinister. The boy was poisoned.

A tiny sliver, the length of a thin match, had pierced the considerable layers of his wet vestments, and punctured his right tricep. The force required to hurl such an object at sufficient velocity a considerable distance to find its well-clothed target was a wonder to contemplate — and with such stealth! We immediately suspected Indians; Castorito assured us there were none, or he would know it.

But the doctor soon replaced the journalist. Upon closer scrutiny of the fatal arrow, I determined it might have been dipped in the juice of some nightshade, of which the forest afforded plenteous toxic varieties; another possibility was moccasin's venom. The boy was feverish, the area about the dart's sting red and swollen; a general ashen complexion had seized his countenance. Working quickly, I administered a generic antidote, and was much gratified to see the patient respond to its salubrious influence within one hour. His color returned, the fever broke. The boy's stupor swerved to the more assuring oblivion of sleep.

Leaving me free to interrogate, in a fit of outrage and growing panic, our stone-faced leader.

"For mercy's sake, Captain, (I exclaimed) I implore you to tell me what in blazes is happening here! If you cannot, I demand that we turn this party back immediately, abandon this parlous Grail's quest before we suffer further losses, whose extent and revocability we cannot predict. I thank the maker your son shall eventually rise from his present delirium, but what of us? Shall we 'scape so easily from the next disaster that befalls us? There is clearly still more to this Gregín, this monster or devil that connives as a man, than I've been told, and as your friend and partner I demand to know all! I demand it! I demand it!"

This venting of choler had a purgative if dizzying effect upon my person. More importantly, the effect it produced in my colleagues, an effect visible even through the moonless murk of the forest, led me to apprehend at last some resolution.

Castorito, with a tantalizing intake of breath, first opened his mouth to speak —

"Vásquez, we ..."

— but the loose-lipped, rodent-like Achilles was immediately silenced by the stern upturned arm of Agamemnon, who curtly instructed him to scour the perimeter, keeping within line of sight. The Indian spat and scurried to discharge the order, rifle in hand.

There and then, seated beside his reposing son (sleep rendered the nubbin's features in an even more childish cast), a disquietingly discomposed Captain Bell began:

"First things first, Juan. Forgive an old man's indulgence. I sought only not to alarm you needlessly — and indeed, dyed-in-the-wool soldier that I am, to test a civilian's mettle on this o'ergrown field of Mars, before imparting our ... well, yes, our secret, our plot and our cabal. You see, eventually you would have witnessed in any case — you *will* see, I assure you, you may stake your life on it ... that the end —

indisputably the scientific find of the century — more than justified the means, the absolute need for secrecy, the machinations of which you, (I am sorry, my friend) have been the dupe. I felt assured that once captured, safely bound and sedated, this creature, our quarry, seen with your very own eyes, would so astound you, so fire your imagination and so move you to marvel at our feat and your fortuitous participation in it, that all these niggardly details of intrigue, of petty finagling and exigent subterfuge, would vanish like the morning dew ...

"So you will agree we acted under the best intentions ... but again I speak obliquely to my purpose. In any case, I see now your own too-sharp mind has overborn the flimsy cage in which we sought, temporarily, to restrain it. Know then that ... well, this is speculation, you understand, but of a sort based on years of research, deduction and copious recent evidence ... know that the being ... the being we track ... but perhaps the relating of one critical incident will congeal the picture into sharper focus ..."

It was with difficulty that I followed the thread of his discourse. The old man's faculties, though prodigious, had been unbalanced by our journey, to a degree I could not measure, leaving precious little that was stable besides the iron core of his objective. But in the recital that followed he quickly recovered his concentration, and did indeed, I must say, astound me with his explosive denouement:

"El Gregín took one of party ere now. Two summers ago, we traversed this very territory in search of the beast. It was some three days ride out of Refugio. Our nettlesome counterpart, a man under my hire — a butcher, by trade — disobeyed me and rode off after the creature solo, I myself having been incapacitated by my startled mount. Enraged at the breach of discipline, I very nearly shot the insubordinate in the back. The details are of no import, but you should know the man was a veritable Hotspur, who, perhaps due to his 'carnal' vocation (I know not), enjoyed the smell of blood and the infliction of petty tortures. He would have yanked the wings off your little bullfinch one by one, then moved on to the legs, the tail feathers, the plucking of the eyes, always ensuring his victim remained alive and sensate to every particle of its torment, before impaling it unto the spit, through the heart, to roast. He was a scamp of the lowest order, a militiaman of the sort charged with patrolling the republic's frontiers (Bell of course described the mercenary bulldog troops known today as the "Texas Rangers," counterfeit symbols of the Texan spirit whom my own countrymen for a thousand reasons despise), but a man whose talents, in this corner of the world, were not without use.

"Well, he met his right end, as all cowards do, on soiled knees. We came upon his corse three hours later, eviscerated, much like those unfortunates we buried, his head skewered from ear to ear by a crudely fashioned spear. A spear, Juan! Gnarled, ungainly, requiring terrific force to transfix its target in the manner that it had turned Pabst — the miscreant's name — into scamp-kabob, yes, crude, but undeniably a crafted weapon! This was the clue, the key that sparked my speculations and set me on course to unveiling the creature's true identity.

"The writings of de Lamarck, the broodings of a hoary southern scientist bouncing around in his *Beagle,* their theories on the chain of being, the natural, dialectic, evolutionary drive to perfection in the animal world, with its countless foiled experiments and extinctions along the way, the still-unknown migratory patterns of fauna across the Bering passage, all flashed like lightning before my eyes ... Juan, do you follow me? Does the same surge of electricity ripple along your spine as it does mine? The answer is there, staring at us, its thick maxilla masticating in our faces! A perfectly scientific elucidation of the Barankawa legends!

"Think of it, I say: it is not some mythical beast we seek, not some rumor or superstitious savage's sprite. But neither is it an animal — yet neither again, is it man! We hunt not *Homo Sapiens,* Juan, not *Homo Ludens* (ha!) — but *Homo Erectus!* Pithecanthropus! It can only be so! A lost, brutish, distant cousin of our race, leagues, millennia from its ancestral home in the dark continent, quite possibly the last of its species, driven to murderous rampage and flight not by mammoths or sabre-tooths, but by man himself!

"Imagine it: a more ... a more ginger Gregín, so to speak (here he chuckled at the anagram), scant years ago, a creature enjoying its inferior brain's concept of natural harmony with its environment, displaced for aeons but settled in its North American habitat — before its gloomier downturn into genocide ... a time when it lived, here, in this very wilderness, at peace with the world, undisturbed by the onset of civilized man. Now it has come unhinged, reverted to its survivalist tactics, its instinctual flight response that saved it once before from eradication a continent away, that drove it to escape with its life at all cost, to return to a land more in keeping with its natural dwelling. To go south, south! Its God-given instinct drives it south, with only ourselves hot on its trail! Make no mistake, it shall attain its haven if it crosses this last river. The vast spaces, the warmer climes, above all, the desolate jungle expanses of your country shall swallow it forever unless we intercede; unless we capture this prodigy now and ... and ... well, my friend, you, a scientist, understand full well the ramifications of such a find — and why we therefore kept its true identity hidden from you. But I have spoken enough. I trust you understand now the earnestness of my devotion to this cause, why it is worth any sacrifice. I trust ... I trust you understand it. I shall assume no more."

He rose, strode off into the darkness, his cane at his side, the most incongruous figure in this wilderness, a ghostly white Prometheus confronting the inky gloom. On this, the final night of our fatal expedition, my courage was redoubled, my lagging hopes rekindled, my fatigue shorn up by an infectious bracing fervor. I knew then, silently tending my patient, that at the critical hour I would be, would be ever, *his* lieutenant.

X. Billy's Dream

"... Mr. Bones ... M-m-mr. Bones ..."

Such did my young charge weakly mumble in his troubled reverie. The boy's eyes shuffled like antic fish in their pond of lids, and a sweat broke out on his temples — yet he had no more fever.

"... Mr. Bones ... don't, Mr. Bones ..."

"A childish vestige of his," Bell explained, after some initial discomfiture. "The name of some bogeyman, a fiend that strangles babes in their cradle. A tyke's vision of El Gregín, perhaps." He smiled. "Wake him."

"Captain, whatever this apparition, it will pass. Better to let the boy recover ..."

"Wake him now."

Billy's mumbles continued, no louder but more insistent: "Don't ... Bones ... we're sorry, Mr. Bones ... do-o-o-on't ... B-B-"

"I said wake the brat!" And he dealt the boy's head a blow, with the side of his hand, of such severity and shocking swiftness that my breath actually 'scaped me. Before I could protest, the lad was startled awake, suddenly bolted up to a sitting position, and with astonishing alarm, and wide eyes, as if his nightmare did not balk at the borders of this reality, pleaded tearfully with the towering figure of his father:

"Paw, please, please let's fergit 'bout this (or something in this vein; I struggled to catch the words) ... please, Paw, we's gonna die, we's gonna die ... it's happenin' again, Paw, it's happenin' again ... we'll git killed, Mr. Bones, he'll kill us ..."

"Silence! Silence, I say! Damn you, whoreson!" And he struck the beseeching figure at his feet a crushing slap, followed by indiscriminate blows with his cane.

I had just managed, after no small struggle, to restrain our frenzied leader when Castorito quickly emerged from the bush, his eyes aglow and wild in the unnerving darkness, and breathlessly declared:

"Captain. It's started."

XI. The Vanishing

The next several hours flash by in my memory; it is all I, a decrepit taxed beyond my years, can do to stay their flight and resolve them now into a coherent narrative. I *feel* this night in my being, this night that fell like a hammer on my soul, more than recall it; the events it brought rush and blitz in my mind's eye, more impressions, emotions, than concrete pictures, as unto the fluttering wings of some great bird that swooped down from the heavens, and grasped me inescapably in its talons.

Bell booms his commands ... Castorito and I stumble over the brambles to fulfill his order, rushing to form a perimeter, a defense against ... against ...

a fast-flowing stream, the brood of the storm, directly before me, a great gush, blocked here and there by vegetation ... nothing, nothing clear, eyes straining in the dark ... how quickly, how quickly it all happens, a blink of time ...

the dull thud of a swooshing missile, arcing, crashing with its black mass directly on the Indian's head, he screams, I fire my musket at the dark, the crackle all 'round of gunfire ... Castorito still screams, I turn, I see him, to my left, see him holding a misshapen mass, contorted, bulky, mottled ... the dog ... Bela's mangled carcass, virtually ripped inside out, its spaghetti entrails entangling the Indian, who screams and struggles with the dead thing ...

the Captain's voice, ringing out, a maniac's shrill whoop:

"A Bull? You seek to squeeze me in your Brazen Bull? Bravo-o-o! You thrust and parry, ha ha ha! You retreat, you feign, do you? You circle us like a wolf? Damn you to hell! (he fires his revolver at nothing) I shan't be! You hear? I shan't be a Blücher at Waterloo!"

he fires ... unholy noises, an inhuman voice, out of the impenetrable murk, the voice of the darkness, twigs snapping all around us ... my musket cannot find its target ... there is no target ...

eliciting a howl from me, the Captain plumps down close by ... he shuffles up close, his eyes burning, wheezing, his brow atingle with sweat ... he whispers, he sees it, clear as day, he sees it, he has the fiend in his sights, but he must get closer, closer, close the gap, there, there in the riparian grove ...

Billy too converges on our position, awake, adrenalized ... his courage, too, restored ... "I'll go, Paw ... I'll go ..."

the Captain is predictably categorical:

"Stay here, all of you. You have not the vision, you cannot see our quarry as I. Cover me, men. Cover me as I charge ... Juan (in his beautiful Castillian), Juan, my friend, remember this, remember it all, Juan, my baptist, my confess-o-or ... My friend, this is the moment of which most men only dream. Juan, I never told you

of my third and final vice."

"And ... and what is that, Captain? I-I've often wondered of it, t-truth be told."

"It is ... the vice of being an inveterate prankster."

and he charges ... the rustle of leaves, branches, damn it all, I cannot see ... I

cannot ... a struggle, by the bank ... the rushing stream, I cannot ...

one ... one near-word, one syllable, one bare Rosetta glyph ... the captain:

"B —"

a splash ... I cannot ... Billy screaming out at his apparitions, all our apparitions, I

know not what, "You sumbitch! You ain't nothing, you're a gambler, a liar, you

sumbi-i-i-itch!"

and we are running ... the dark implodes ... I cannot see ... I cannot, breath,

wind, trees flying by, their legs, their legs pulling ahead of me, swallowed up ... I

stumble, drop my musket, recover, chase after them deeper deeper deeper in the

wood, I cannot ... Billy's voice again:

"Buddy! Buddy, we give up! Stop i-i-i — "

cut off abruptly ... twin screams ...

run, run, trailing, run, I cannot ... see ...

I come upon them, my last seconds of life:

a large pit, two flailing worms at its bottom, screaming, spikes of gore through

the Indian's leg, a pit ... camouflaged ... camouflaged ... a tra —

The left hemisphere of creation explodes,

my eyeball bursts,

I am dead.

XII. Credo

All birth, all life, the Buddha wrote, is suffering. As my soul parted ways with the abyss — all red and speckled turbidity, opaque, impenetrable, rubbery smoke — on its, my soul's, return to terra, I felt that bodily suffering — what ineffectual things, words! — I felt it clench and suffuse the whole of my being. I was swinging, that was the first tidbit of my restored awareness; swinging from a branch, a hanged man. Hanged by my arms, hogtied, my head an unspeakable shambles, by the light of a fire I saw ... it.

I wish to, I must, describe this being in detail.

All the color of soot (only its eyes and darting tongue reflected the campfire's glow), it had protruding lips, orbs that burned yellow and glaucous, twin flaring voids for nostrils, cheeks a moonscape of clefts. Ruined teeth bent at odd angles, housed in gums set back in a misshapen jaw, tongue absently flicking from corner to corner of the mouth, the creature focused on coaxing more flame out of the fuel it had flung. An ancient brand, a large "B," had long before been cruelly seared onto its temple; a keloid of such bulk had accumulated there, about the ruined skin, as to nearly impart upon the being a unicorn-like aspect. Wooly hair of pitch, longer in some parts than others, shot off in all directions from an unevenly round head — but this disheveled mane was hardly "black fur that shimmers like the Nile in the pallid light of Dian's moon"; rather it was a tangle of debris and dirt, indeed the whole of the creature's body seemed a wondrous walking microcosm of the wilderness; the unnatural and bare feet, too, were encrusted with mud, stray vegetation — and blood. The thing was dressed in rags, through the rends of which were clearly visible, even by campfirelight, the knotted furrows of lashings without number, most ghastly on its back, where they formed a twisted, intraversible mountain range, but evident all over the torso, even on the normally tender skin of the lower gut. There and throughout, the entity's skin was the texture of sun-scorched hide. Suddenly it turned from its labors, pleased with the fire's glow, rose to its full height and faced us. My heart, notwithstanding its many recent ordeals, leapt in my chest. This prodigy that loomed before me, sinewy and powerful and terrifying beyond words, this dun-colored Golem seemingly carved out of Gibraltar itself, stood a good two heads taller than the tallest of our party. Momentarily its glowering orbs melted me with the unconsidered gaze a lion might assume towards the lowly pismire, then the creature strode over to one of our company's packs, strewn on the ground, kneeled down once more and commenced to rummage through it. Its huge, wrinkled hands (the merest flick of which had dashed out the ripe grape of my eye) quickly emptied the pack of its sundries, then threw it into the flames.   I noted one other feature of this being as my senses returned: it reeked appallingly of feculence. Yet even through one eye, through the intense pain shooting up and down slung-up arms, through the mounting horror of my situation, its (in the end) incommunicable beauty was awesome, awesome to behold. A commensurately indescribable thrill of fear and tenderness rippled through me. I felt almost as if in the presence of some fantastic lost titan of Olympus, of Eden, of the Mesozoic, of — but of course *El Gregín* was nothing of the sort.

Acromegaly? The man — for man it was, I thought — suffered from this condition of giantism; thus I surmised. Hence the oddly shaped feet. Lame, the wretched being had probably been kneed, his left leg tendons cut, to discourage flight. As these musings burst like fireballs in my brain, I all but trembled entire, reeling to the pith of my soul at a reality my mind refused to accept.

Tearing my gaze from the spectacle of our captor, I turned to inspect my surroundings, and ascertain whether I was the only crew member yet among the living. Indeed not. Next to me, hanging by his wrists from the same branch of sturdy post oak as was I, his feet bound in identical fashion as my own, was Billy. The boy had clearly been awake for some time while I was given over to oblivion, but speechless; he cowered in terror, his curiously naked legs a quivering white blur. The unfortunate bantling had been much abused: his lily skin mottled blue, watery rivulets of blood snaking down even from his nether regions. His coat of many layers hung in tatters that clung to his upper torso, but left his lower extremities exposed — he must have been strip-searched. The boy's futile struggles to free his arms from the rope evidently only brought on severe cramps in his limbs and shoulders. On the ground lay Castorito, whose groans doled out a throbbing basso to the fire's soprano crackles and tenor pops. (I had mistaken the sound, I realized now, for the lolling of wind.) The Indian's legs had both been pierced through by multiple spikes at the bottom of the pit. He was slowly bleeding to death, in unimaginable agony, yet caring little for that; his frequent lip smacks and dry darting tongue suggested to me that the pitiful brute, infant-like, yearned only for his bottle.

This had been appropriated by our captor, who sipped liberally from its contents, absently spat his own sap into the fire, and knelt examining an object he'd retrieved from one of Billy's innumerable packs: a Bowie knife. My searching eye had taken in all this within seconds, yet what I could not see was the glimmer of a solution to our plight.

Suddenly, quickly, our jailer got up on his feet, approached the knife's owner and, with the graceful stroke of an orchestra conductor — an odd analogy, but it was just so — El Gregín lopped a sample the size of a walnut from the boy's cheek. He screamed, cursed, though I noticed the chirping of the crickets was undeflected from its melody. The side of the boy's face gushed a mask of red.

El Gregín — Mr. Bones — but let us call him by his given name, Buddy — held the specimen of flesh between thumb and forefinger, examined it as one would a species of butterfly or fossilized bone, placed it in his mouth, masticated the vile food, and loudly swallowed. Then I heard, for the first time, this prodigy's voice — deep and alien and awe-inspiring. The voice, like rolling thunder, addressed us, one and all:

"I eat you. I shit. I shit you."

Despite his buccal gush (though extraordinarily painful, such a wound would not prove fatal in the short term), Billy bargained with our jailer for freedom. His promises and apologies can be imagined, as can the indifferent response from a creature that held us so completely in its power. This being stood before us, its lanky limbs like trunks of gnarled, solid oak, and pronounced its awful sentence:

"You're'll pigs. You pigs die. You judged. You die."

He staggered back to the fire, suddenly clutching his side in obvious pain. I read its source as I would an open book (as my remaining orb also spied the handle of Bell's revolver, tucked into the creature's stained trousers), yet I shuddered, overcome by a deathly ennui, an acute sense of futility and desolation. My brain, my every limb, pounded a dull ache that served as counterpoint to the searing fire in my smashed and gored socket. Better, I sighed, closing my lid and relaxing in suspension, to surrender. And yet I refused to die ignorant of the precise symptom that had brought me to this pathetic end.

"B-Billy," I mouthed weakly through a parched, defeated throat. My voice was hardly recognizable. "Billy. Why ..." (Castorito involved in his own private torments, I had to address the boy in my disfigured English.) "Tell ... me. Why you say ... Gregín ... Why?"

The boy, breathing quickly, only noticed my entreaties after several seconds. Ropes creaking, he swung his head to face me.

"What?"

"Why? Tell ... why ... Gregín."

His countenance compressed into a painful sneer. His eyes, heavy-lidded, pierced me with cold contempt.

"Dumb git ... It was nigger we was after. Nigger runaway. *Ni-gger*. Stupid ... stupid Mex." And he dropped his head in exhaustion.

It was this moment, my brothers, that I would look back upon in subsequent years. Inscribing these words before you, an old man, I am transported back to that night of my rebirth, of my arrival at true understanding. For it was in that single instant, I avow before God and all my comrades in the cause, in that shining moment of revelation, that I learned to hate. To hate purely, to hate discriminately, yes, but to hate. To hate what had to be hated — I saw it now! — to remove all obstacles to the mission and leave behind the middle road: this was the only way. I learned now in a lightning bolt of inspiration that hate could be shaped, molded. That it could be used as fodder for a cannon, to batter down the ramparts of darkness once and for all. Hanging literally by a thread, half-alive, trod down by the full weight of an apathetic universe, I was seized by the insight that hate could be turned to constructive purpose, to instruct and illumine, to clear the path to the blessed, irrevocable truth. With that comprehension, that plucking of reason's boon, I was remade. From the blighted depths I reemerged, whole and steadfast; I saw my course, that single course from which I've never strayed; I knew in that instant that for all the life still left me — be it minutes or years — I would know where I must go and what I must do. For the first time, I was truly, unambiguously alive. I was born again. I saw my struggle.

Reanimated, I sought an audience with our captor. I pled not, neither did I curse. I merely explained, calmly. I trusted in reason, in composed intercourse between compeers, to pull me through. In the best phrasings I could manage in his language, I appealed to the conscience of my tormentor.

Buddy.

These men have duped me. Though you've no reason to trust in what I say, and may find this difficult to credit, I had no intimation that we were pursuing *you* all this time. A man. A man. Christ forgive me. I was duped, Buddy. I was duped. I stand ... I hang before you here, shamed to the core of my existence to have been party to this execrable campaign. Buddy ... My name is Juan. Juan Bernabé. I am a journalist, a foreign correspondent. I am the eyes and ears of my countrymen. I accompanied these villains what seems, what was, a lifetime ago only to report on what I took to be a legitimate expedition, a journey of discovery. Indeed it has been. This is tragic. Tragic. All of it. Buddy, you must believe that I meant you no harm. I will die a broken man unless you confirm it. This violates ... violates ... Buddy, my government ... my people are friends to your race. My country boasts several enclaves of escaped slaves living on the border and in the interior. You ... you must know that. Hence your flight south. Oh, God. You seek release from this hellish land that has cursed and abandoned you. Release you shall have. We are near these settlements and your freedom now. We welcome with open hearts our black brothers from the North, freshly escaped from bondage. You must believe me, Buddy, when I say that this has all been a mistake, and I swear to you that I will write about this outrage in my paper at the first opportunity, if I live. The world, this wicked world of pain and sorrow, this damned worst of all possible worlds, shall hear all. See, see these human tears of remorse I shed before you. See that I am your brother, brought low before your mercy.

I am a *fuereño* *. I owe no allegiance to these deceivers. These white devils. I hate them now, I know that. Buddy, I am a learned man. I am training to become a doctor. You suffer from cholera, do you not? You have been losing liquid all these several days, you burn with thirst. The dehydration brings intense pain in your abdomen, is it not so? The Rio Grande lies near, the frontier is almost within your grasp, yet the disease appears advanced. It can kill swiftly if untreated. You may not reach friendly civilization before it strikes you down. Let me help you. You need water. Dispense with Castorito's poison. Take water from my pack. There, in the hidden pocket, you've not exhausted our stores. There is soap as well, if you'd care to wash. There is an extra canteen, there, at the bottom. Drink it, not too quickly. In my medicine bag, yes, there, the black leather one. Drink it down. Good. Feel its coolness quench the fire in your loins. Keep it by your side and drink often. May Christ in Heaven forgive me, forgive us all. You must stem the flow of fluid from your body. Your system cannot handle the diarrhea indefinitely. Look. Look inside the alligator pouch. The one with the golden clasp. Within you will find a small reddish vial. If you cannot read, it is labeled with the shape of a mouth making the sound 'Oh.' That is raw opium, for the relief of your pain. My laudanum is gone.

----

* Literally, "outsider," used of Mexicans not native to the northern republic.

That is opium. I do not ask you to trust me. I do not ask you to spare me. I ask only that you let me help you. That you let me ease your suffering. Take a small amount, it will speed you to a relaxed state where your pain will recede to a dulled horizon. You doubt me. Here, give me some if you do not believe. I will take it with you. I will do whatever you command, just believe me that I am a doctor and a brother and I want to help you. Here. Give it me.

There. You see? It is opium. Opium. A man named De Quincey called it the ladder of earthly bliss. Yes. That's it. That's enough. Take it. Ingest it, thus. Yes.

You recognize it, don't you? I have heard the poppy is not unknown in certain reaches of the Dark Continent. It will relax you, bring you relief, without dulling your senses. Not in this amount. It will serve only to soothe you. What? What did you ...? My friend. My friend, you move me. You do not need to thank me. Here in this dark wilderness, it is my kindest reward to see you better. To see, oh, holy mother of God, to see a smile return to your parched lips. Believe me, you tormented creature, the Job of your race, you who have suffered unspeakable agonies for so long, believe me. Believe me when I say that not only my oath as a physician, but my own incontrovertible nature, binds me to relieve the pain of all downtrodden creatures such as you.

Buddy. Buddy, hear me. We have not done all. You still require a preparation of glucose solution to combat the cholera. I have the necessaries in my bag. The water will not suffice, you are only releasing it as soon as you swill it down. Buddy, for the love of God, you must let me prepare it for you. It is glucose. A simple mixture of solution and glucose, but in the improper ratio it might poison you, bring about nausea. Untie me. Keep your gun on me, I care not, but untie me so that I can prepare the medicine for you. I will take it first , to show you, if you don't trust me. I can withstand the foul effects, but your condition makes losing any more fluid dangerous. I will take it if you do not trust me, so you will see it is not hemlock. Let me, for God's sake, let me! I see you still suffer, and you are still losing fluid. You are a man, a man! You are not beast or chattel. Use your mind. Your mind. You are dying. I am the only one here who can save you, with one quick preparation of what is in my bag. You are a man, Buddy! Shoot me afterwards, please, if you like, but let me help now. I ask not for my life, understand me. My life, everything I believed in, is dead and blasted and finished. I ask only to deliver you from your strife. You, only you, are all that holds meaning for me now. It is your life I must save, not mine. Understand me, I beg you. Understand that I love you as a brother. Untie me. You do not have to die.

He wavered. I pronounced with all my heart to do nothing to harm him, that his real foes had already been dispatched; we were completely his. The very sight of him, I said, filled me with loathing for the beings who had led me on a such a damnable "expedition." He had to take a leap of faith. Form a bridge of trust between men. Have faith in another, use his God-given intellect to make contact with his fellow man, who had so long abused him, to reconnect with another human soul, an act that is the peak and summit of human compassion, that which raises us above beasts. This, I knew, was in his power as a living, thinking *human* being. I said many, many things.

"You stinkin' Mex," Billy suddenly shouted. "I knew you'd backstabbin' us the first chance you got, just to save your stinkin' skin, you goddamn darkie bastard —" And he uttered several other curses with which I was unfamiliar.

"Shut up!" was all I could muster in retort. "You lie to me! You take ... take advantage of me, of my ... of my ignorance! Scum! You go to hell!"

Buddy found this exchange rather amusing. Perhaps the opium enhanced his perception of this truly ridiculous sight, his two remaining pursuers swinging, spinning slowly by their wrists like beasts, yelling at each other, slabs of chattering meat. Castorito, meanwhile, lay stretched on the ground, softly murmuring what might have been his death song.

Buoyed by this exchange, Buddy released me. He kept the pistol trained at my head, but his manner was already friendlier, more relaxed. He did not fear me. Even if I were to turn on him now, his massive form and superior strength could vanquish me in an instant. After all he'd seen, done, survived, dispatching me would have been child's play. Indeed. Through the slight muddle of the opium, he could easily crush me with those huge misshapen hands, wrought of iron by a lunatic Bernini, break my neck with one blow, or simply shoot me. No one would hear; this forest was desolate, desolate for scores of miles.

I prepared the solution. He asked me to hurry; his pain was beginning to break through the opium. Unfortunately together we had consumed the entire, piddling remnants of my stores; yet my own dose had now smothered the fire in my eye to throbbing, glimmering embers and imparted a sensation as of a million needles prickling my joints — a feeling which spurred my hands' legerdemain movements all the quicker. I worked quickly by the campfirelight, telling him it would just be a couple of minutes more. My heightened senses recoiled at the stench of his pants, the murky water dribbling out of his bowels, that great, bleak physiognomy enlumined by his arched brows of hope.

I completed my task; my companion shoved me aside with one prodigious paw and, ignoring Billy's ire, my whispered "Cheers" and the Indian's song, the slave in one gulp downed the drug I'd so assiduously and exactingly concocted.

The effect came about within perhaps one minute. He spasmed and fell, dropping the pistol. He convulsed for perhaps thirty seconds, then quieted on the ground — paralyzed.

I stood over "Buddy," gathered some sputum in my mouth, and released it into the basilisk's black astonished eye.

Belladona atropos.

I had calculated the dose precisely to incapacitate but not kill, not immediately.

I quickly untied Billy and Castorito, rousing the Indian with a preparation of nonlethal atropine. Aside from his mangled legs, he had a mild concussion, though with the aid of my elixir he would remain conscious long enough for my purposes. I stood erect before my stunned companions, addressed them in a bemusedly military tone not unlike that of the absent patriarch.

"Right. Gentlemen, let's be about our business. There's not much time; we've perhaps five hours 'til the morning light. We've a mission to carry out by then. Castorito. Leave your bandages alone. Pay attention. First things first. Ask Buddy where we might find the Captain, dead or alive. You heard me. Ask him."

"He ... he says Bell was washed away in the stream. He's gone."

"Is that so? I see. Vanished from this earth without a trace for daring to gaze on that awful visage. I see. Hmm. Well. The Captain was ... Castorito, interpret! The Captain was vanquished by water; therefore another element, a more ethereal one, nearer to heaven, knave, shall serve for your dispatchment. Nearer to heaven, aye. Or to that other place. Hmm. Hmm. What to do. Do you hear me, wretch? I believe you do. Listen well. I could shatter your neckbone with my musket, but that might render your body numb to what is in store. And we shan't have that. We shan't have that. Castorito. Tell him. Explain to him word for word what I'm about to utter. I want ... I want it to know what is coming. I want it to know. *I want it to know.*"

The Indian did as commanded. I was never so eloquent, nor the Indian so hard-pressed to interpret my words, but a full catalog of my intentions was eventually conveyed and we soon set about our task.

The demolition we visited upon that body over the course of the night would hardly yield to a description from my pen, nor can scribblings of ink denote the sacral nature, the curiously magisterial, religious fervor that pervaded our work. We banded together, a united brotherhood, to systematically and utterly destroy a creature purporting — daring to purport — to belong in our company, an upstart species impudently tapping its claws at the gate of *Homo Sapiens*. This demanded a swift and unequivocal response. No muscle, therefore, no nerve, no district of flesh was left untouched, undepraved and uncorrupted in this new nisus for obliteration, this palpable casting out from the house of man. I cannot, as I say, render effectively the profound unmediable reality of our salvationary act — the contrary of crime — hence I will restrict myself here to a brief sketch, to give the reader — it is my fervent hope — a faint flavor of the proceedings.

We opened and closed with fire.

Knowing the belladonna would soon wear off if we tarried, leaving us once more to the tender mercies of the beast's superior strength and viciousness, we set off immediately. Under my direction we heated the machete (the very one, it turned out, which the fiend had applied to the Texian family — and poor Bela), in the campfire. This set the instrument at a proper temperature to impart a searing sensation to the serratus and other muscles as we clove the creature's four limbs messily from the trunk. I performed the actual slicing, chopping, slicing, chopping, wiping off the dripping blade after each amputation, flinging each loosened, still-spasming satellite into the flames, whilst a bandaged Billy followed close behind to hold a cauterizing torch to the stringy stumps. The last thing we wanted was our patient to bleed away ere the final act was played.

Suitably incapacitated, though rendered unconscious by agony, we strung up the head and trunk upon the very branch we had ourselves so recently adorned, and inspected our handiwork so far. The upper arms were neatly separated at the shoulder, though I 'd inadvertently cut through femur on the lower left limb. (dear Dr. Bünter at the institute would have understood, I'm sure, given the crude, improvisatory nature of the conditions.)   The blackening offal, meanwhile, sizzled loudly in its own curdling fat, the flames now frantically stoked to a bonfire by Castorito, under my orders.   The ignited logs and branches, still humid from the storm, produced much sulfurous haze that blotted out the night, shunted the campfire's glow to the redder reaches of the spectrum. The stars eclipsed by our blazing, fuming limelight, we sweated profusely on our hothouse stage.

Act II. I roused the wretch with more atropine, which now wholly and assuredly served counteract the soothing effects of opium, and we spent the next few hours composing a *chef d'oeuvre* of destruction on the bare black canvas, each of us making suggestions, laughing, jeering, feigning, egging the others on, building up to a frenzy of artistic excess, a rococo of torment. The great Buonarotti in his chapel could not have felt a more profound inspiration than that which buoyed our merry crew of dabblers that *notte*. Again, I hardly need go into much detail here (my narrative, I feel, has gone on quite long already!), but a pair of examples should suffice to convey the species our feats.

Castorito, in a bit of heartening invention, called for the victim's ears and nether regions to be removed as keepsakes, an Apache habit that neatly segued with my own ethnic penchants, our cult of the matador. Capital, I said, capital! We did the deed, eliciting a gurgly scream apiece. I struck upon the novel strategy of utilizing Billie's Bowie knife (that most quaint of Texas instruments) to perform an ancient rite: the evisceration and removal of the still-beating heart as an offering to the sun god Quetzalcoatl. (Never mind we were performing it at night.) Yet before I could assay this move, Billy stilled my hand, his breath reeking of Mescal, and proffered one last ceremony I could perform with my doctor's lancet.

Perfect, was my response.

We three stood solemnly around the lightly swaying, gore-steeped figure before us. The crickets chirped in unison, sweet music for our industry. We gazed upon our handiwork, long and hard. Bubbles of liquid sputtered weakly from split nostrils, emitting a low wheeze. Its hair was almost totally singed off the deformed head, the experiment of our young aspirant baker. Its crowning "B" blazed in beads of sweat, an ancient talisman, the mark of fate. The scarlet letter. Ye Gods! This laughable, misshapen lump sought admission to the league of humanity? Never! Nothing could be more ludicrous — this our operation had plainly shown. Lancet in hand, I addressed the odious remnants of its blasted face.

"For the innocent family you slaughtered, brute" — here I slit a quarter-inch diamond from its cheek, handed it to Billy;

"for the Butcher you slew" — another star-shaped portion from its temple, delivered to the Indian on the turf;

"for our noble Captain, whom you so unsportingly and cravenly dispatched" —

a last piece for me, the fruity pulp of its lip;

"for your countless and cowardly crimes, we consign you to be consumed. For all this" — here we each chomped, chewed, swallowed the communal wafer, the word made flesh, in imitation of the fiend:

"we ... shit ... you!!"

And then only, this last office complete, did I proceed to the Bowiaztec *coup de théâtre* — the last thing its remaining Cyclopean orb, hanging by a thread, would ever see.

And yet one thing gave me pause, at the very cusp of my matador's stroke, one thing and one thing only had moved me, oh so briefly, to belay my duty. Looking closely a final time upon the shattered monster's countenance, I saw, mingled with its juices that glistened in the excited fire's glaze, I saw ... tears. The abomination wept. But this elicited merely a momentary shudder, a frivolous fermatina. A trick of the light. My creed was enacted, our cause embraced, the deed done.

In cadenza, we cast the Dark Prince into hell. Though we could not, with our limited means, urge the fire to the requisite 1,000 degrees that would consume a body outright, by a combination of alternate burning and physical battery we steadily whittled the melted and charred remains down to sooty coals of intoxicating redolence, some the texture of fatty wax, others soughing the crackle of crumbling marrow. Our composition, like unto Orpheus' strains, brought forth a flaring artificial sun, warm and dazzling and beauteous to behold. All the while, mine orb abrim with the fuliminating spectacle, I heard such lovely notes — aye, and with new ears, my dear reader, with the ears of the newly born:

Dies irae, dies illa
Solvet saeclum in favilla:
Teste David cum Sibylla.

(I noted the Indian, too, seemed to hark this spectral euphony; he struggled weakly on the ground, against his wounds and his drunkenness, to flail his body in a native dance, all the while mouthing his savage's song.)

Quantus tremor est futurus,
Quando judex est venturus,
Cuncta stricte discussurus!

By morning only the heart, that stubborn mahogany of the corpus, remained. Yet this too, in united and devoted commitment to our toil, we progressively stomped to powder. By first light of that first day, that first fabulous dawn of my rebirth, all traces of El Gregín were effectively obliterated from the earth.

XIII. Epilogue

There is little left to tell. We separated, Billy and the Indian back to the north, I by foot to the bosom of my country. I was done with Texas, my cradle; important work, a mission suited to a man, awaited me at home.

By bright morning light, my parting with Billy — at last denuded of his many layers, robbed of his night-imparted grandeur, the scrawny sprout seemed even more lost in a unkind world — was awkward, given the fact that our interpreter lay dumb on an improvised stretcher and our exchange was reduced to broken phrases and gestures. But his neurotic insistence on knowing one thing struck me as characteristically bizarre. He kept asking whether I had "seen what Buddy done to him" while I swung on the tree; unsure of his question, disoriented by the night's exertions and the odd patina of the moment, I could only mouth, "No, no ..." and shake my head vociferously. Satisfied, he nervously smiled, briefly took my proffered hand and staggered off on foot, dragging the Indian behind him, out of my life forever.

I later discovered that Castorito, who soon slipped into a coma on his makeshift travois, did not survive the return journey. To this I append no comment.

My struggle continues to this day, the struggle to bring my country to reason and reverse its policy of damned acquiescence and coddling towards the slave — of whose true nature it remains disastrously ignorant. Yet surely the outcome of the raging conflict to the north, that mortal engagement over the very soul of a divided nation, shall sway our short-sighted leaders, our politic whores in abeyance to the Gaul, to rethink their views. I have therefore set down this, my testimony, my credo, so that the country of my fathers may learn from my lesson, take from my experience, gaze with my lone piercing eye, all the more efficacious and apprehending for the loss of its brother. I write to spur on the Confederacy, that noble knight of sovereignty, swinging its flaming sword at the criminal elements of the unnatural North, a North that would have man and monster balanced on justice's scales. Never! say I. Never!

I recently received a letter containing the fate of a certain Major William Charles Bell of the First Regiment of the whooping grays, killed in action along with his commander, the revered Col. Bushell, in proud defense of his freedom at the Battle of Mansfield. Let the blood of these martyrs serve as a spur to our mission, the sole true mission of all right-thinking, liberty-affirming men. Despite the grievous loss of our comrades in arms, note that this day in the crimson-splotched fields of Louisiana was ours, ours! Let this blessed victory multiply, and carry to the gates of Washington itself the rallying cry: "We shall overcome!" Our cause, our struggle, is

God-ordained, my brothers, so let us "screw our courage to the sticking place and we shall not fail!"

And lastly, to my progeny, those unknown sons and daughters of pure blood to whom I have addressed, aye, bequeathed this testimony — remember me, remember this lesson, remember my cause. Above all remember your undying, inescapable heritage!

Magna est veritas et praevalebit
in saecula saeculorum!

— Translated by F. C. Bart
Brazoria Agency,
Austin, TX
January 18, 1986

Belinda

April 8, 1998

From: Belinda Brenham
       167 Bastrop Lane
       Austin, Texas 99847-0099
       USA

To: Raul Robledo, executive director, Navarro Family Archives (ret.)
       88 Avenida de los Insurgentes, Apt. B
       33985 Ciudad de México, D. F.
       México

Dear Señor Robledo:

I'm writing because I heard that you were ill, and wanted to let you know that we wish you a speedy recovery.

I also wanted to render you a belated apology. While my father, Senator Vasquez, was alive, I did not dare endanger his fragile health, but now I suppose it doesn't make a difference, except to you. I am sorry for my father's behavior towards you during that Testimonio affair back in '86. He had no right to cause you so much trouble, when none of what happened was your fault, and in fact you tried to prevent the document from ever leaving the archives.

It was long ago proven that it was in fact that horrible man, the translator, Bart, we guess egged on by my father's political enemies, that added the horrible details to my ancestor's story before absconding with the text. Well, wherever he may be now, I hope he feels some regret for the terrible trouble he has caused us all. That is between him and his god. But my father was so angry, I'd never seen him like that, ever. I suppose he needed someone to blame, a scapegoat, and you were it. The whole stupid, horrible business, I'm certain, led to his heart problems.

But I know too that what Bart might have added to the document did not take away from the central veracity of the translation or significantly change the Testimonio's content. J. B. Vásquez was an evil man, a monster, really, who fought long and hard against the equality of blacks and other "mongrels," as he so atrotiously put it. I know that. I understand that. I can face that. My father couldn't. Raised on family legends and stories about our "abolitionist heritage," I guess the stories were just too important to him, too central. He couldn't stand their being proved false.

So accept my apology, señor, for everything. I wish you only the best.

                                        Sincerely,
                                        B. Brenham

P.S. I have enrolled in Spanish classes at Austin Community College for the fall.

Deepest night.

*Paris can be astonishingly silent at a certain hour, almost guiltily so.
Two texts, or agglomerations of texts, remained, one ensconced in a
creased and rubbed manila folder, the other – the burned one – caged in
its own large envelope.*

*Both these latter manuscripts were bulky, more heterogeneous, than the
first, which had required merely a rubber band to hold it together. But its
sisters were virtually spilling out their disordered, variegated entrails onto
my coffee table, straining against their bonds as if eager to disclose
secrets too long kept.*

*It was with care that I raised the manila folder to center court, pushing
aside its predecessor. Before beginning, I caught sight of a short note
scrawled in pencil on the folder itself, evidently a clue to the text's
decipherment. Its counsel:*

The three parts can be read in any order, or all at once.

*I scratched my oily curls with an olive finger at this riddle, and opened
the folder. A noiseless wind stirred the windowshades. What wonders!
One portion of the text seemed printed on the oldest, most decayed paper I
had ever seen outside a museum, while another chapter's presentation I
found entirely novel: the words appeared to have been impressed on a
pinkish paperlike substance through some vehicle other than a printing*

machine. The off-black script almost seemed to pulsate with electrons. I had never seen the like.

On the quietest, darkest night in Paris' memory, I trained my black eyes first on the ancient text, fearful it might come apart in my fingers at any moment, crumble to powder at the slightest breath ...

MOTHERLAND

You hold in your hands a literary marvel. The correspondence of E. G. Chrevova has long held a treasured place in Russian letters, and the sensation engendered by their publication in that fabled, tragic land in the year 1821 can scarcely be apprehended by our present sensibilities. But thanks to extraordinary efforts on both sides of the channel, the denizens of Albion's shores can at last share in the amazement, the romantic fervor, the flood of emotion and wonder unleashed by this small collection of letters.

Small, I say? Yea, small only in girth, verily! This modest batch of missives - and its dizzyingly baroque addendum - have inspired philosophical debates, ideological treatises; they indeed opened the floodgates of the ongoing "Women's Question" explored so capably and movingly in the nimble hands of that fabled, tragic land's social giants, including (to but name a few) Chernyshevsky, Dostoyevsky, and the divine Tolstoy.

E.G. Chrevova, the spotty record shows, was a noblewoman consigned to a cruel lot. Her brother, Prince Konstantin Gennadievich Chrevov, was an important figure at the court of the recondite Empress Catherine II. Yet the childhoods of this worthy pair were an unending parade of ghastly horrors perpetrated by their father, Count Gennady Konstantinovich Chrevov. The princess, upon the mysterious death of her father (mysterious only in the official records of the time, but its truth is revealed here, by God, revealed here!) quit the belle monde of her birthright, abnegated most of her fortune, and fled to the East. There, in a region of fabled Siberia (to which the noble survivors of the Decembrist revolt would soon be consigned to three decades of hard labor by a cruel

Alexander II), Chrevova slipped into a hermitess-like existence, unknown even to the serfs bonded to the area.

She fostered a reputation as a madwoman, alone and mysterious (no more, by Jove, no more!) in her humble dwelling that, like its mistress, withstood several winters until her baffling disappearance sometime in 1793. Her shelter provided no clue: it was burned to the ground. The humble plot of land, aside from a blasted heath where the hovel once stood, held only a modest grave to mark it, its stone illegible and abandoned.

Whatever the princess' fate, could she have known, the makers of this humble tome wonder, could she have guessed that the letters left behind, eventually bequeathed to the famous Kamensky archives, would set off a literary firestorm? Would she have apprehended that her correspondence and its enigmatic addendum (its origin unresolved here, alas, alas) would become a classic of visionary literature? That it would drive at least Russian critic stark raving mad?

For surely no document produced in our enlightened epoch - let alone any other produced in the previous century - could equal in bizarreness and *outré elan magnifique* the novelty of those 10 pages. Product of a fevered womanish mind? Sign of precocious literary talent? Conspiracy of letters in Russia, that fabled, tragic land?

We leave it to you, our esteemed readers, to decide.

F. Bart

London, 1888

94

Translator's preface to the second edition

Time's cruel arrow has affirmed the validity and steadfastness of this humble

tome. We need not add here to its multifarious accolades. While perhaps not the

huge literary watershed its previous publishers hoped for (indeed, demanded)

The Correspondence of E. G. Chrevova inspired the imagination of many a

discerning reader in that foul season if its release.

This new edition means to satisfy the public's hunger -still-smoldering, surely -

for the undeniable charms of this relic from that fabled, tragic land to our East.

Time's cruel arrow, alas, has pierced not the dark veil of mystery nor shed any

more definitive light on the case of the resplendent E.G. Chrevova.

Subsequent research in the Kamensky archives only confirmed the bewildering

enigma of her fate. Her brother, Prince Konstantin, seems to have arrived at this

very conclusion. Upon chancing to read her correspondence many years after the

fact, the prince had the peasant woman, Proskovia -- herself already aged and

decrepit -- brought to him in Chrevovkino to answer to the mystery. The account,

though suppressed, was somehow preserved in the Chrevov family chronicles as

set down by the literate peasant Khramovkin, and later endowed to Count

Kamensky:

> Where is she? asked the prince of the crone, now almost completely deaf.
> To the woman's protestations of ignorance, the prince applied the age-old
> techniques of interrogation so widely practiced by lords and governments,
> eliciting only the groaning response, "She died. Everybody in the *oblast*
> regards it so. She perished in childbirth and the house was burned by
> brigands. So the story runs." The wretch of woman expired soon after in
> agony, never to see her native land again.

So the mystery remains, despite such simplistic, unsatisfying *denouements plus non-magnifique.* The makers of this humble tome sincerely wish the public will seize upon this volume, so modestly priced, for the treasure, literary and artistic, that it truly is, and give it the most prominent on their shelves for years to come.

F.C. Bart, Esq.

London, 1897

August 11, 179--

Sir --

The potatoes ripen ahead of the coming frost, I spent all morning turning the earth about them and preparing the plot for cabbage -- the peasant woman Praskovya having lent me her *sokha* [Russian plow -- F.B.] -- the sun bearing down in a sky of crystal, birds like daggers lodged in it, with Praskovya's Lyonya arriving promptly at noon to reclaim her *sokha* -- she has ten children, they live in the Kuklivo estate nine versts away [1 verst = 3500 English feet or 1.06 km – though on a slog through the quagmire of Russia's nonexistent country roads it feels much longer – F.B.] -- the boy refused water and departed, while the daggers cawed and the potatoes swelled in their wombs of root, I am happy. This I report to Pronya, swelling in his own little subterranean womb by my plot, his gravestone weathered seven years and the flowers I brought him 69 days ago wilted. He said the potatoes keep him company and together they sing "Lev the Mouse," just like we did as children. You tell me Moscow will burn and that pleases me.

 I have sorted it all out, and I agree. Upon my return here I heard the bee-moan buzz of the device *[ustroistvo]*, saw your letter spilling out as I presume you intended and you presume I intended to intend to presume. The third letter --

but of course the first -- greases the matter and settles the affair in my estimation.

Yes, I say. Yes, I say.

Though I must say categorically at first I felt rather puzzled. Your answers to

questions I had yet to formulate -- yet somehow knew that I would -- thrilled to a

degree you can, I am sure, scarce imagine. My questions to your answers still

more so. But those letters are gone, as you intend, as I presume you intend, and

further I delight to agree, sir, to your offer. All is clear and Pronya concurs.

Kostya and Papasha I care not for. "God is in heaven and the Czarina is far

away," as the serfs say. Indeed so. Indeed so. Do women really go about

hairless, in flowing robes of floss? How very amusing.

August 30, 179--

Sir --

Odd indeed, indeed, indeed, to take pen to paper after such a long period of
neglect. The habit of it, the memory of the feel of my clammy fingers about the
quill, it had all quite escaped me. The posies in the forest are in bloom, along
with the jeering moss and laughing fern, the loose-lipped toad tells me I am
damned and should hold no conference with you. After working in the plot I
ambled in the glen near the peasant dwellings, heard their wretch's screeches of
song across the stream. Turtles danced on the water's surface. The mazurka.
Mother would glide across the parquet, my father holding her as if she were
made of glass. A caravan of caleches -- Kuklik's brood -- slithered up the path
towards the main road. Their season here over, the peasants sing. Kostya I
never saw at these gatherings.

You ask me to describe my life. Your recent letter (it is difficult of course to
determine the sequence), before its words vanished from between my fingers,
proposed that I tell you of my past. Quelle idee tres charmant. I must say, sir,
your Russian is exquisite, taking into account you are a foreigner and hail from a
land where, you say, my tongue is long dead. "Incorporated." A rather material
description, say you not so?

The peasants brace for winter. Joubert is tossed onto the embers, howling, jackal-like. You invigorate me, sir. I have not roamed, traversed the forest shadows, swimming through clouds of *pukh* [airborne mold, quite abundant and intolerable in Russian summers -- F.B.] with such elan, such animation, with such animation, animation, as I do now, not since first arriving in Irkutsk oblast. Alina spits on his ashes. A curious sensation, sir, for one such as I, so long departed from society. You tell me they all live in oval glass houses that reach deep into the sky. Your country, sir. Your country. My condolences for the mark on your forehead. I once saw Papasha rip the nostrils out of old Arsentiev's face, for not paying his *obrok* [quitrent]. We went indoors and ate strawberry cream, brought specially by Arsentiev for the children. And yet you say you know me. Curious.

 But tell me, sir, this odd device you've made a gift of and rooted on my "drawing room" table. Of what does it consist? Its smooth white contours reflect no light, yet it glistens clearly. Its cooing reassures me in my bed as the stove's warmth lulls, log crackling, howling like a jackal beneath me in winter. Its knobs and red eye sit deathly mordant all through the day, but spring to life as I feed my letter into its narrow mouth, which slides open with unearthly, quite unearthly, frightfully unearthly, motion, motion, motion to receive it. Can you elaborate upon its origin? And why it spits it out like an unruly child, I was an unruly child, Kostya pinches me, Pronya sing me "What is Summer." Every journey is static return.

September 2, 179--

Sir --

Impatient, I plucked a potato sleeping from its bed and half-devoured it, tossing the remnants at Zuyev's brats who'd come to have a jeer at my expense. They made me quite happy. "Baba Yaga! Baba Yaga!" they yelled from across the meadow. Tonight I had potato soup and fell quite ill. Your postbox's buzz revived me. It pleases me that Moscow will burn.

I read, yes, I read. Sir, how come you to this knowledge? The sequencing has corrected itself. As a very young girl I entertained quite a passion for young "Werther." A peasant girl, one of Praskovya's issue, was found drowned today in the Chita pond. Her hair -- beautiful hair, past her waist, aspiring to root itself in the soil -- had caught in some branches beneath the water. The corpse was found mauled by a bear, a fishing bear. Joubert said she was a stupid girl to bathe alone in the river. Praskovya concurred. Feliks cut her free -- crows flew in all directions -- and let the bald girl float away free downriver, her flowing skirt undulating like fish.

Kostya and I returned to the house for the Easter meal, happy to break our Paschal fast. The house was a flurry with servants and relatives, dashing about, preparing the meal. I insisted on helping, though Maman laughed, "You are only five, Zhenya. Your place is not in the kitchen. Go play with your brother."

101

But when she wasn't looking, when she conversed with my aunt Philomena in the drawing room and supervised the setting of table, I watched over the *kulich*. [Easter cake, conical like a scone and exceedingly bitter -- F.B.] I assured Ksenia, our family cook, sir, reared in her craft in Germany before I was born, you should know, I assured Ksenia I would mind the *kulich* while she went and attended to some activity at the *devichei* [threshing barn, where many stores were kept -- F.B]. I stoked and stoked and stoked the flames, the waves of heat sprouting sweat all along my face and down my back. The *kulich* was blackened and burned to a crisp, sir, the kitchen and house stank horribly. After dinner Joubert flogged Ksenia mercilessly. "Ruined!" my mother cried. "Ruined!" We children watched from the window, my cousin Julie showed me her dolls from Geneva, but Kostya watched the spectacle outside, with the peasants, while Pronya played a merry waltz on his guitar. I do not know where he learned it.

September 15, 179--

Sir --

Happy to hear from you. My appreciation for the many queries addressed. I share everything with Pronya, and he is much amused. In your world he would be a freak, I suppose, much as he is in mine. Yet only he could speak on equal terms with Papasha. Such is the custom in my barbaric country, sir. The *yurodlivy* [Russian holy fool, a notoriously difficult institution for foreigners to grasp, though perhaps the recollection of the liberal license granted to Lear's fool by his aged king would give the reader an approximate idea of this relationship and its bounds -- F.B.] holds a high place in the family hierarchy, unlike the peasants my father would compel, say, to stoke his pipe. They were often replaced for some minor infraction or other, or none, sent into service in the army by my father on a whim. But my, these "hippolyce" are enthrallingly funny. But I am boring you. This morning I awoke violently ill; the potatoes languished in their cribs. Afterwards I carried the contents of my stomach to feed into their sweet open beaklets.

    Are you quite sure I cannot know your name?

September 19, 179--

Dear Sir --

The period I address, you should know, was at the height of the "Pugachovschina." You insist on knowing this, but it is but nothing. But nothing, I say. Old Arsentiev was weeping over the death of his dog Platon. The dog was found hanged from a willow, its eyes gouged out. It had also been -- but no matter. Kostya was in an affable mood, and to torment me he described how he'd plucked out the animal's orbs, how he -- My brother, sir, you must understand, serves at court. I fled Petersburg, our estate at Chrevovkino, I -- but no matter.

September 29, 179--

Sir --

This morning woke and despite my nausea went on a long constitutional through the glen, skirting Alkanovo. Light scintillated off the dew-wet leaves, a galaxy of day stars all about me. Two boys herded their sheep in the distance. I walked on. Winter nips; she sinks her fangs into the district; I hear the work of the mines nearby. I have never seen Irkutsk. A little girl, with a basket of berries I meet on the road tells me the city has grown as more ships float in and more exiles flood the barracks. I have seen them, trundling along in chain gangs, sir: gangly-bearded men, in rags, their eyes deeply sunken and black.

Papasha -- sir, you should know, I must tell you this, though you cruelly refuse me even your name -- my father, I say, sir, is a vicious roué. Plagued with the sickness of my countrymen, of the malaise that penetrates the nobility to the core despite Catherine's reforms -- I should say indeed because of them: debaucherous languor. Papasha quickly made his way up the ranks and married my mother in her 16th year. The two combined fortunes were quite considerable, and upon my brother's birth the family lived at Chrevovkino, outside Vyra, most of the year. By the time I was born, mother had resolved to stay at the estate as much as possible while Papasha spent much of the time traveling, looking into his affairs at the other estates and currying influence at

Petersburg. I never ventured from Chrevovkino until my fourth year of life,

living instead in a bubble of domesticity with Maman and our many serfs -- my

father owned some thousand souls at Chrevovkino, more at the other properties:

my *nyanka* Pelageya, me and Kostya's tutor Bunt, a surly German who

eventually drank himself to oblivion, and dear, dear Pronya. I first saw him --

this I remember -- standing over my crib, staring down on me with his one-eyed

gaze, humming "Katyushka Matyushka." He entered my world through song.

Dear, dear friend. The soil now muffles his music, but it reaches me still.

And then there was Joubert.

How very odd, sir, and sad, too, that your letters evaporate like a lethe-soaked

dream. That I could hold them close, to read and reread as missives from a

faraway friend. There is something transmitted through them, that I cannot say

what. Perhaps you can enlighten me. The sunsets lie stretched out as if on the

rack, straining and heaving against winter.

September 30, 179--

Sir --

A brave new world, indeed, that you describe. Yes, I am fond of the "Lettres persanes." Yet I can hardly credit this image of woman. It seems a gross arabesque. Your words of course have vanished again and Pronya calls me and I cannot concretize this idea further and I am distracted by burrowing roots but these ... what did you call them? These "matriarchs"? A jest, sir. A solid jest. I too have read "Emile" and I cannot credit it. Oh, who are you? What is your name? It is a world where Rousseau lies strangled and Voltaire, in the shape of woman, lords over the serfs.

October 23, 179--

Awoke.

Stored preserves.

Polished the postbox, though unneeded. It seems somehow to repel the dust.

Pronya speaks not to me. Angry?

Sir, I am unwell.

I walked and walked through the forest, returned well after dark. *The Babye Leto* is not protracted in the East. Winter descends and the cold freshens me. The valley white with the first snow. I am ready for it. Well-provisioned. My thoughts. My thoughts. The *Babye Leto,* sir, is our last glimmering of sun before the onset of the dark. But why need I tell you this? You know everything about me, about my country, my century, my life, do you not, sir? You read through me, say it. *Babye Leto Babye Leto Babye Leto.* The English call it "Indian summer." Bunt taught us some English. Siberia knows no Fall.

November 5, 179—

yes yes yes yes yes yes yes yes yes yes yes yes yes yes yes yes

yes yes yes yes

yes yes yes yes yes yes

yesyesyesyesyesyesyesyesyesyesyesyesyesyesyessssssssssssssssssssssssssssssss

December 21, 179--

My husband --

Honest, honest indeed you have been with me. Yes, yes, I agree. Provisions will keep me through the winter, worry not. I have borne many others, I cannot count them anymore. Winter revives me. A peasant's frozen carcass in my potato plot, a bottle fused into his hand. With Pronya's help we dragged it to the edge of the meadow, where the serfs will take it.

I have kept your account in a safe place, as you asked. Still I do not understand why this message should linger while all your others evanesce within minutes. Your words are like strong roots that anchor me to this world; I cling to them in my memory, recite them -- but I do not write them down. I obey you, my lord. You have made me yours and we will serve you.

There is much in your strange *povest* ["account," though with the tinge of a longish narrative somewhere betwixt the English "novella" and the Spanish *cuento* -- F.B.] that eludes me, I do as you ask as you ask as you ask, sun of my winter. Pronya stirs not, cold in his grave, the potatoes broil in my bowels.

My mother died when I was 10. Kostya and I had heard the rows between our parents, when Papasha would drink himself into a stupor and the peasants fled his wrath. Kostya enjoyed the floggings and multiplicitous cruelties and indignities inflicted on the servants, of course -- he and Joubert often assisted my father in them or went off and started their own bouts of torture -- yet when father started beating him too the matter of course changed.

Our house was a tense, excruciatingly tense place -- as I have said, it was during the Pugachovschina. My father cared not at all.

Though he forbade his children to play with the serfs' little boys and girls, it was of course simplicity itself to evade his gaze, even when he started spending more and more time at home.

One day Praskovya whispered to me in the bathhouse -- she replaced my usual bathing girl due to the latter's infirmity with child -- she whispered, all atremble: "He murdered the mistress. Strangled her with his bare hands as he would a serf." I did not want to believe her lies -- my first impulse was to have her flogged, along with all her brats for good measure -- but as the days passed I knew it was so. I spoke with Kostya about this in his room (he was three years my elder, and though rather womanish and delicate, was developing into a beautiful young man, resplendent in his lyceum uniform, and after the whole affair his charms took him high in the ranks in Petersburg, in the court of the Empress, where -- forgive me, I interrupt myself), I told him the peasants (I knew well not to identify which to him) were spreading this rumor, and with a cold stare he turned to me from his writing desk -- this writing desk I am using, in point of fact; I had it brought here from Chrevovkino -- he turned to me, his face blanched from the powder, his wig fresh with pomade, I associate the smell with his statement to this day, with his eyes unmoving, boring dully into me --

he turned and said:

"But this is old news. Haven't you your precious dwarf to go play with?

Can't you see that I'm busy?"

I insisted on the matter, quite ... quite distressed, and he seized me by the arm.

Hard.

"You can never know what man is. Our father is a man, nothing more. As am

I. As am I. You know nothing. Now go and play with your goddamned

dwarf."

I am reading your *povest* and familiarizing myself with my role. We will fulfill

your charge, my love. We will. I can feel you moving inside me.

February 27, 179--

My Husband --

Dreadfully, dreadfully slow it goes, deciphering this *povest*. But what I read alarms me in extremis. Your letters sustain me through my fright over these nightmare futures. And yet I enjoy the flames. Moscow will burn, you say, and that pleases me, sitting warm and content in my far-away *priyutechka* ["shelter," though with a notably tender inflection -- F.B.] torn from Russia's orbit and so near, so near to you. And yet leagues, centuries divide us. And then your words, bridgelike, close the gap again. Oh, would that you were here, with me, away from that prison of your era. But I am being atrociously sentimental, and of course, inexact as woman. For you are here with me, day and night, smoldering in my thoughts and swelling in my belly.

The valley and forest indescribably lovely under their mantle of snow; the faraway mountains like hoary peaked goliaths watching over us, the wise elders of the earth. By the light of the stove I reread Karamzin's *Liza* [*Bednaya Liza* (Poor Liza), Nikolai Karamzin, 1721 – F. B.] and caress you in your nest.

113

March 11, 179—

My Husband –

That evening at Chrevovkino in its final year, an evening both typical and signal to all our fates. Papasha, besotted with Arsentiev's *samogon* [home-brewed spirits, ordinarily ghastly to palette and corse -- although I've had the good fortune to sample some in Kaluga not without its charms. The traveler to the Russias is advised to stick to pure-grain vodka in any case -- F. B.], seated at his imperial dais in the sitting room. Kostya, myself, whatever servant girl he has taken a fancy to at this point tightly leashed at his side (I hardly exaggerate the matter). The liquor and debauchery aged my father before his time; though only fifty he looked much beyond that. Dribbling onto his frock coat, his wig disheveled and cocked, he watches as Pronya sings a merry peasant song and all of us assembled chime in with suggestions for verses. Joubert has long since been borne away to his room in a stupor. I stare at the servants; the fear, the contempt in their eyes underneath the merriment unnerves me. Only Kostya and Papasha do not see it. Are they blind, like poor Arsentiev? They are. They do not see the explosion coming from the Cossack south, spreading through the empire like a constellation of sparks on brittle, brittle grass.

For all this, the entertainment is capital. Pronya is a master with his ditties, his wordplay. Dressed as Arlecchino, he gambols and pirouettes to hilarious effect

114

as the musicians try to keep up with his wildly darting stanzas. He is clever, so

clever, the light of intelligence and humor burns in him, a fundamental

humanity, a dog star to guide me through so many seasons of despair. For me, a

girl of 13, my childhood is long dead.

  In the frenzy of his performance, Pronya -- his distinctive walk exaggerated

now as he thrashes his stubby arms about in hilarity -- approaches my father,

who has slipped into oblivion on his seat. As the servants gasp, he climbs onto

father's lap, in order to reach his wig.

  "I will show you our new lord!" he tells the crowd, improvising a song.

"Stout of frame/stiff of mien/A shining, hairy sword!"

  He removes the wig. My father remains insensate, his shiny pate pale and

blue-veined, like a newborn's. Back on the floor, dancing and tossing the wig

into the air, Pronya screams out his ditty, "A shining hairy sword, I say!" and -- I

cannot imagine what devil possessed him -- pulls down his trousers and plants

the wig on his ----. To general astonishment and roars of laughter, the dwarf

marches like a dragoon across the floor, arching his back, swaying his barrel-like

body so the wig remains in place. "All salute our new lord!"

  Kostya roared along with the servants at this outrage; he had grown to hate

Papasha in his months home from the lyceum.

  Father did not wake to witness this scene, nor do I believe it would have had

any lasting effect on our lives – but for Joubert.

The steward caught wind of Pronya's tomfooleries the next day, and reported them to my father in the most unflattering tones. I repeat that father allowed his *yurodlivy* all manner of license -- you surely know, my love, of the unique, sacred and inviolable bond that unites the master to his *yurodlivy* -- but the Frenchman so stoked my father's ire, so fueled his easy vanity -- that the latter gave Joubert license to exact retribution.

Joubert and his henchmen caught the dwarf, my dear friend, in our topiary park and -- this was reported to me later -- excised the offending member.

"'Eat it!' the French cur told me. Swallow it all up!'"

This Pronya reported to me, far from the house, by the river, on our first walk after his long and painful convalescence. Winter was licking at the leaves. His eyes were desolate, their shine dulled, while his body had thinned, shrunken appallingly in only six weeks.

"How could this happen?" I cried. "Why would he allow it?"

Pronya held me in his embrace, I sitting on the grass, he leaning unto me in sad repose.

"'Tis so, Zhenya." This was the whole of what he would say. "'Tis so."

                                                        April1, 179--

My lord --

The time draws near. I can feel it. And I shall not fail.

Spring creeps timidly in; no sooner do the icicles start to drip from the branches, than they are caught once again, like rabbits in paralyzed poses. Winter, a cat toying with prey, relinquishes her jaws only gradually. Yet she cannot touch us.

The remainder of my past, the last leg of this long inward journey you've lulled me on, my heart, is perhaps the simplest to tell. To tell. To tell. Pronya tells me his grave is cold, cold as that night of our emancipation. "Shiver'ing in pieces in a snug little space/My parts lie together but not all in their place!" he sings.

The estate was in turmoil. The serfs who had not run off, emboldened by the Pugachov rumors -- as indeed all of the Russian peasantry was at this time -- demanded redress from my father for his decades-long abuses. None of this however, would have mattered. Uprisings were quelled throughout the country as soon as they sparked, then and now (and there and then with you, my love, as you report). But for Kostya.

My father's penchants, it had been long known in Chrevovkino, had strayed from young girls exclusively as he aged. At the same time, his battles with my brother intensified; as the old man withered, dragged down by wine and a lifetime's excesses of cruelty, so did the young man's claims on our diminished but still vast holdings rush to the fore.

And so came the day -- infamous and gilted -- when screams in my brother's chamber drew me adash down the corridor after a long walk in our park. No one seemed about; the house was terrifyingly empty. I burst open the door -- and saw Papasha practicing his penchants on Kostya, Joubert eagerly, his visage insanely alight, holding my brother in place.

It was not long after that. After what I witnessed, after what they had done to Pronya, I knew it would not be. And it will not be long now, my husband. I have your instructions committed to memory. I've entrusted your *povest* to Kulikov -- he was quite shocked to see me in my finest livery, come to call. They returned only in the last week from Moscow; the roads will soon be untraversible with the Spring thaws. He was shocked, I say, though of course he knew of me; he served with my uncle in the cadet corps and it was not difficult to secure this favor. I am, though a mere woman, still a noble after all; and despite the recent stains to my family's reputation our holdings have prospered under Kostya's management.

It happened in darkness, on the cusp of winter. At the agreed hour, we all gathered -- servants, farmhands, Pronya, Kostya and myself -- on the front lawn, under the birches, in our fur coats and galoshes, to watch as the house sparked and ignited and consumed itself in flame. Joubert, howling like a jackal, leapt from the balcony, the fire snapping its claws at his feet. No matter. The peasants dragged him back, bearing him up above them like a conquering hero, and cast him through a window's melted glass. Alina spat on his ashes. Pronya and the musicians led us in a merry ditty as the mansion burned and released its spirits to the blackened, starless night. Kostya did not speak, merely stood there, stone-like, the shadows dancing on the scowling rictus of his face.

We never did espy Father trying to escape the precipitous destruction of his tiny world, nor did our ears catch any screams or cries for help from within the swirling holocaust. But by morning's kinder light, as he later told us, Kostya came upon Papasha's scorched and blackened remnants where his palatial bedroom once had been. Senseless as ever from drink, the old man had likely never even been roused by the terrible inferno that consumed him. We three felt less than nothing at this news.

The horrible "accident" brought letters of condolence from all ends of our vast acquaintance. The will was executed with dispatch, the property meted out. My sole condition to Kostya was that the serfs be cared for in perpetuity, their countless abuses brought to an end; upon this promise I kept my silence. He of course eventually reneged on this agreement, once I 'd quit his life forever. But Russia is as she always has been, my love, the pith of cruelty.

Pronya I managed to save. Society holding nothing for me, despite my riches, I convinced him to join me on a flight from all we had known -- into virgin land. Our necessaries were embarked, and three hard months of winter travel brought us to the frayed edges of the empire, to the frozen shores of Lake Baikal. This

was ... but I have lost sense of how long ago.

April 15, 179--

My love --

We are ready. He comes. Know that I trust you and have faith in the justness of our venture. Be strong. You are the only man I have known -- though in truth I have not known you. Yet know that I agree, that you are my lord and master, my nameless overlord. The postbox is swollen, unpetaled, moaning and warm to the touch, ready to receive its charge. To receive us, carry us, somewhere, somewhen, anywhen, foreverwhere, so long as it be to you. Until we meet, my love. Until we meet. Until we meet.

E. G. Chrevova

could have ever known.

Bart, a pitiful alcoholic, labored in the shadows of the London literary scene, jumping into one quick-money scheme after another, spending his meager earnings on drink. This pattern continued until his death (he fell off the pier in Brighton, dead drunk according to witnesses, and drowned). This "Correspondence" was almost certainly an elaborate hoax.

Though certainly not elaborate enough for Bart's tastes: the garish, fabricated story rightly failed to capture the public's attention and disappeared into oblivion. Today the book is completely forgotten, both here and in Russia – if indeed the Slav race ever knew of the "opus" to begin with. The alleged Chrevova's letters have never been found.

Did Bart smuggle them out of Russia, or were they, like him, a total fraud?

After dropping out of the languages department of Hampstead college, Cambridge, Bart – who was no more an "esq." than I a martian – traveled across the continent to elude his creditors, who were never far be-

curious case of F. Bart and his odd
production was seized upon by the
Theosophist circles in turn-of-the-
century St. Petersburg, where it is
said the original letters did in fact
turn up.

The 19th-century literary critic K.
Maximov, who wrote for the *Herald*
in the 1860s, was lionized in this
circle. Maximov allegedly claimed,
just before a total mental breakdown
from which he never recovered, to
have cracked a mysterious "code" in
the very language of "The
Correspondence"; these encrypted
passages allegedly revealed to him
not only his own future but that of all
persons associated with
Chrevova/Bart's work.

The last note in his diary, scrawled
in a progressively illegible hand,
states: "Everything, all commentary
to the letters - including my own,
dear God, my own - is encoded [?]
into these [?] God God [?] ... doomed
[?] .. of the gyns [??]."

If this be so, then the writer of this
humble commentary certainly hopes
he has been quoted accurately and
in full ...

Another curiosity of that age,
though perhaps one not quite so
fantastical, nonetheless proved far

REPORT TO THE JKH80 COURT,

887IOI]XMCJH PROVINCE, DISTRICT 490JD, NEW ATALANTA

IN CASE

MATRIARCHATE VS. "GENE NELSON"

BOADICIATTA 35, 04JKD9,

0930

PROSECUTRIX GYN-E86876, CHIEF AGENT FOR THE MATRIARCHATE,
PRESENTING FOR THE GOVERNMENT AS PER STATUTE 937IUEB (CHPT.
308HFKJ, SECT. XXXCW54) OF THE GAIA COUNCIL PENAL CODE.
THE STARS AND BLESSED LUNA HERSELF BE WITH US.

ARBITRATRIX GYN-Y82D0 PRESIDING. LINK ESTABLISHED.

REPORT FOLLOWS.

Sisters:

I stand before you, at New Atalanta, site of the first victory of the New Cycle, carried out exactly 5200 lunacykes ago, to argue for the UYTYU-866 of the last vestiges of XY terror. A fortuitous coincidence, is it not, that here, where the gyns first rose out of the shadows of their age-old Oppressor those many moons ago, we should all convene in the Gaia-link to ZZZ.009iu its last traces of infamy? For such do I accuse the accused of being. Infamous. Its crime by this late date is well-known, every child, even on the far reaches of dark Europa, has heard of it by now. We have even be apprised that unrest may be concomitating from these extraordinary events. Monstrous! Horrid!

Detestable and unspeakable as this 9ufazwq is, our steadfast unity and ovariance in the snout of it must be clear, our decision swift and immediate. We ...

Say the charge!

Say the Say the charge!

Say the Say the

I hear your clamors, my sisters. The court hears them. We are a just institution. The Martyrs did not lay down their bodies that we should violate their principles. We shall

itemize the charges in accordance with our code
89rhare08jgfjg0486uyuyuy-70.

Be it hereby declaimed before this court, this jury, before
all Gaia herself, that the XY-099 "Gene Nelson" - the vile
fiend would not allow any other designation to be coded
into the datalinks - stands here accused of the following
charges:

* that on the evening of Theresia 16, LC 5043 N.C., it
first knowingly and willfully initiated an illegal
manipulation of the chronobanks;

* that for that purpose it consistently stole ameliartium
from the New Atalanta Center for Space Travel for over 100
LC;

* that during this mindlinkerape of the chronoVeil it
maliciously and abusively LLL-0099 a helpless pre-NC gyn;

* that in consequence of such foul deeds, through ... I can
barely speak the words ... through non-43085jfkdnLKH
methods performed on this defenseless sister, illegally
produced an XY.

I hear your gasps, your cries of outrage, my fellow Gaians.
Painful as it is to admit, the Matriarchate permitted this
crime, perpetrated by a lowly XY-099, out of - may the
Matriarchs forgive us - a long-established and secret
alliance with the traitor.

"Nelson" - how odious, how guttural do these pre-NC
designations sound in our Enlightened Era - this XY-099, it
can now be told, was chosen through genescan to consult on
the Euridycette674-iuf33dn8 project, specifically in the
area of engineering. "Nelson" was thought a thoroughly
clystered XY-099, its primitive brain unclouded by hormonal
occlusion, violent behavior or Oppressive tendencies.
Clearly, the genosurgeons at its production had done their
usual exemplary job. But something went terribly, terribly
Plklhjk99.

**THE PROSECUTRIX CALLS FIRST WITNESS: GYN-398IDJHG8, CHIEF
SCIENTIST, NEW ATALANTA SPACE RESEARCH CENTER, HEAD OF THE
EURIDYCETTE674-IUF33DN8 PROJECT.**

TESTIMONY FOLLOWS.

Yes, I thought it was horrible. At first. I protested

mightily to the board when they first brought this ... this

"Nelson" to work amongst our team. "Are we returning to the

Dark Cycles?" I asked them. "To the days when gyns and XYs

mingled together, when we fought and warred and suffered at

the hands of brutes? How can we allow this in Our

Enlightened Era?"

0944 O-DIRECTIVE O-DIRECTIVE O-DIRECTIVE O-DIRECTIVE

AS OF 0944, ENUNCIATION OF ACCUSED XY-099 SELF-DESIGNATION

RENDERED ILLEGAL BY NEW EMERGENCY LEGISLATION O-DIRECTIVE

99-00767778UUT.009, SEC. MMM9898776767, PAR. 786-YY. YOU

HAVE BEEN INFORMED. THE STARS AND BLESSED LUNA HERSELF BE

WITH US.

Yes. So, the council would not listen to me. The E

project was ...

WITNESS WILL CLARIFY.

Oh, Guadaloop, 328YTU. The Euridycette674-iuf33dn8

project. The Euridycette674-iuf33dn8 project was too

important, they said, we had a window to meet, the first

chance in over ten thousand lunacykes, the first
opportunity since the DC, to rendezvous with
Euridycette674. We needed N ... the XY-099's expertise.
What could I do? I 679000+-ioed the plan, pledging to the
Council of Matriarchs that I would do my best to work with
... it.

The day it came the whole center was in a shudder and work
proceeded only with difficulty. Even though only a tiny
percentage of our workers would be exposed to the
consultant, allowed only the absolute minimal necessity of
contact for the project ... Euridycette674-iuf33dn8 ... to
proceed apace, still the rumors of this XY-099's appearance
flashed like heracleite through the entire center sublink.
When delivered to my cubicle by the hippolyce, I unshackled
it myself, to show who was mistress. It was ghastly. Of
course, I have XY-099s at home, for maintenance, but they
never stay longer than needed for their chores and in any
case I am not there when they come. And when you see them
on the streets they are of course shackled, shuffling back
to their cells, usually well in the distance. I can
honestly say that never in my life had I seen one up close.
And now, here was this thing, before me. Its revolting
gangly growth of hair protruding from its snout, its empty,

watery eyes, its sheer massivity, standing a good dian taller than me ...

"Is it safe?" I asked the hippolyce. Even in the presence of these armed, superbly-built gyns I was un3zz.

"Don't be alarmed," it said. I felt as if a wave of cold H2-0098 had splashed me in the face. The ... the XY-099 ... it spoke. The lieutatrix instantly punched it into silence, split its lip. It remained stolid, unresisting. I had ... of course, I knew that they could speak, I'm sure I must have heard some mumble a few contrite words to me before, but ... but this XY-099's voice was calm, even, it was ... intelligent. It looked me in the eye, those blue orbs, that freshly-beaten face, they had something in them besides malice, besides cold, brute XY thoughts. I was quite shocked. "'Merciful Gaia,' I told myself, 'what are we getting ourselves into?'" The hippolyce merely glared at the thing, their biceps threateningly tensed, and handed me the papers to sign. This process took several minutes, while the XY-099 was allowed to roam about my cubicle. I was signing the fifteenth form - forgive me, I don't recall the precise nomenclature - when that eerie, low voice spoke out again.

"Catherine," it said. "The second."

The hippolyce turned on it, unsheathed their ova-rods to neuroshock the twice-insubordinate creature, but I waved them still. The thing was now legally in my care. "Y-yes," I said to it, agape. Only I knew to what it had referred. The XY-099 fixed the holoframe on the wall with its gaze -- it had not even reacted to the hoplice -- its loud breathing even and deliberate as it stared at the portrait. It was one of those ubiquitous holoportraits that adorn the walls and line the corridors of all our public buildings, the holy icons depicting matriarchs from antiquity. "You are ... interested in pre-NC chroniclasions?"

It did not answer to my specific query, but said only, "Pugachev. Scared her." It smiled, sadly. In astonishment, I realized its expression had almost sparked my sympathy. Yes, I realize that is an infraction. 328YTU. But it was obvious from this scene that something was very XZ581. I immediately had the XY-099 taken to its quarters. When the hippolyce lieutatrix asked what our exchange had meant, I told her, matter-of-factly - presuming her ed-level would not be high enough to appreciate my answer - that the XY-099 evidently had studied Dark Cycle herstory, that Catherine the second was an ancient matriarch, from whose name that of our own month of Catria is derived, and that Pugachev was a "dissenter" whom she had UYTYU-866ed. "So it's glad to be here?" she said, grinning, and walked out. Evidently irony is not taught at the Hippocorps.

PROSECUTRIX GYN-E86876: Latter remark to be struck from the record, jury disregard. How did the XY-099 perform it duties?

WITNESS: Superbically. Nel ... it was a tremendous aid. Its grasp of quant**876hgh mechanics proved invaluable to the mission. I ... I can honestly say that I had never met a ... person with such capacities.

PROSECUTRIX GYN-E86876: Chief scientist, the martyrs did not lay down their blood so that we might praise the work of beasts above our own. Strike latter, jury disregard. Witness is clearly under stress and will receive treatment upon completion of testimony. Would you repeat?

WITNESS: Of course. 328YTU me. With the XY-099 limited ancillary support, our team had the engines operating at 70 percent above design capacity, six camelias ahead of schedule. Nel ... I mean ...

PROSECUTRIX GYN-E86876: gyn-398idjhg8! For Dworka's sake, remember your oath! You continue to invoke the XY-099's own self-designation! Strike! Strike!

WITNESS: 6416YTU me, Prosecutrix. But the XY-099's designation is a matter of public record.

WITNESS WILL CLARIFY.

Your III-89, mine was not the first department which the XY-099 had "consulted." I verified this when I accessed its file. Its IOHN0-99700. I read there about its polymath background, its self-taught rise from the slums of Somnus, New Tyche, and even then I suspected that this story was a ruse, disinformation it had somehow entered into the link to cover its tracks. The truth is, nobody knows where it came from. It had a perfect service record, that was all the Matriarchate seemed to care about. It had, over at least the last 65.178 lunacykes, worked on numerous projects throughout the Academy of Sciences, some of them secret, ordered and executed by the Council of Matriarchs itself. It is my understanding that this XY-099 had even enjoyed quite a good deal of autonomy on some of these

projects, a fact that shocked me at the time. Over the
course of its ... career, the XY-099 grew so pvnf97 as to
stipulate that it be called by its own self-designation,
"Gene Nelson." Under duress, and under orders from the
Council, I so acted. Before its - how should I term it? -
departure, "Nelson" amended the datalinks to incorporate
its - as it called it - its "name" into the linkbanks, and
to this day our specialists have been unable to remove the
designation. So it should, I would hope, be understandable
that "Nelson," except within the confines of this court,
has become the nomenclature associated with this ...

SUFFICIENT CLARIFICATION.   PROSECUTRIX WILL PROCEED.

PROSECUTRIX: Strike preceding from linkcast. The jury
will note from witness testimony and affidavit (dscjmbn67-
678) that the accused consulted with the Euridycette674-
iuf33dn8 project for 8.576 camelias, under a great deal of,
as the witness puts it, "autonomy." When did you suspect
the XY-099's illegal activity?

WITNESS: To be frank, not until long after it was too
late. ---- - I insist on using that designation ...

PROSECUTRIX: It will be stricken at each instance. You will be held under www457.pki after testimony and treated. Continue.

WITNESS: ---- proved quite capable of disarming me after our first encounter. I put ... it to work on the Euridycette674-iuf33dn8 engine matrix Uoo08965jhfdrw7b-55%%8, where it soon doubled our efficiency. It was not until much later that I realized our energy output had actually increased much more than that, but was being partly diverted ...

PROSECUTRIX: And this is what led to your discovery of the accused's dabbling in pre-herstory?

WITNESS: I believe it somehow got itself assigned to this project specifically to access the LHHK-000. Great Ate herself would not have dared meddle with these forces -- but ---- did.

PROSECUTRIX: Yes, every school child is aware of Dr. gyn-77iugfmp0's revolutionary discoveries in tempor876** mechanics and their application to off-Gaia travel. But it took an unethical creature like an XY-099 to rupture the chronoVeil ...

WITNESS: So it seems. Yes. I blame myself. I grew to trust it, its manner, its words ... You see, we shared an interest in pre-herstory, the Dark Cycles. I have held a lifelong fascination with it, and once I accepted that this XY-099 had been allowed access to the cliobanks by the Matriarchate, that I could speak to it as a ... Well, it disarmed me, as I said. It ... It was only the (ha, ha) -- the timely discovery of these documents that keyed us to the truth. It's my fault. Please, do not KKer-3678 this helpless young gyn. She wasn't aware of what he could do. Please, she was masa in his hands ...

LOGOCRIME. LOGOCRIME. LOGOCRIME. LOGOCRIME. LOGOCRIME. LOGOCRIME. LOGOCRIME. LOGOCRIME. LOGOCRIME. LOGOCRIME.

PROSECUTRIX: Witness is hereby excused, and cited for logocrime. You will be held under www457.pki, YYY.6000ed and kept under observation for 13.035 lunacykes pending review. Bailixx.

Sisters, do not judge gyn-398idjhg8 too -02uty9. It is clear from her testimony and affidavit (dscjmbn67-678) the sort of pressures placed upon her by this despicable XY-099 drove her to the very treme of gyn endurance. The Matriarchate's next witness, sadly, has suffered even more under the perfidy of this fiend, and has become unbalanced, pagliated, 55tt.

Before calling her to testify, the Matriarchate submits evidence exhibits **A-0098uu** and **B-0uy88**, discovered by the witness as part of her student research in the cliobank archives, div. 95jtgjgjgi, sec. 99iusaasa, qud 99077y, on Aphrodeis 3 of this solocyke and submitted to this court on Eris 30. The exhibits document the accused's crimes, detailing at length and in its own words its XXQ-23 and eventual LLL-0099 of a helpless pre-NC gyn; the documents further provide subsequent substatiantion of the crime by pre-NC scholars; and prove the damning charge of chronocrime (OO-PP??) by the accused's depiction of this very trial.

EVIDENCE SUBMITTED.

THE PROSECUTRIX CALLS SECOND WITNESS: GYN-Y677T34, FORMER HERSTORY STUDENT AT THE NEW SELENA UNIVERSITY COMPOUND, 9085TRJKFJ PROVINCE, DISTRICT 990-Y.

TESTIMONY FOLLOWS.

Yeah ... I guess so. What'd you ask? No. No. Where's --
----? I want -------!

PROSECUTRIX: Friends, you will show compassion, I am sure,
for our little sister here, so recently ppot-009ed by the
nefarious rogue XY-099. Her imbalance since her abuse at
the hands of the monster have compelled us to **8899t her
testimony to obviate further logo infractions.

WITNESS: No! ----- you! ------ you! I love ------! You
can't -----

**WITNESS TREATED WITH **44-TU. COURT RECESSED. RECONVENE
AT 1055.**

COURT RECONVENED. WITNESS TESTIMONY FOLLOWS.

I wasn't the first to find them, you know. Back in the DC,
the letters were pored over by tonsa critics and scholars.

I suppose it must've been some oversight of the M's, that
the clio division never knew what it had. Ha. They had it
stashed off under "Pre-NC fiction." Ha. ---- fooled 'em
just like ---- done all along. Anyway, only a fraction of
that stuff is left now. I guess you'll be wuornosing it
now, like you do everything else.

WITNESS WILL ADHERE TO PRECISE NOMENCLATURE GUIDELINES.

328YTU me. You will UYTYU-866 it. It doesn't matter. It
never did.

PROSECUTRIX: Strike previous. Tell us, little sister, what
you did upon your discovery of the documents.

WITNESS: I read them. Right under the M's ----ing noses.
I read about ----, about Evgeniya, about the whole thing,
about this trial -- about these words I'm saying right now.
I read right up to the end.

PROSECUTRIX: And how do we know you're not just acting
(HH-0067) these words, posing for us and for your sisters
in the jury?

WITNESS: Well, then, I guess you're acting too.

PROSECUTRIX: I now call the jury's attention to this
exchange, reproduced verbatim in the XY-099's document, as
indeed is reproduced verbatim the entire contents of this
trial, including this sentence, as evidence of chronocrime.

Chronocrime! Chronocrime!
UYTYU-866 the beast! UYTYU-866 it!
The blood of the Martyrs demands it!

PROSECUTRIX: Your zeal is worthy, my sisters. But the
accused must answer first and foremost to the charge of
LLL-0099 of a helpless pre-NC gyn, as well as to its
maleficent endangerment of this poor unbalanced sorellice,
before moving on to the chronoVeil violations. Such is our
code, sisters.

Tell us, gyn-y677t34, what you did after reading the
documents.

WITNESS: I sought ---- out. ----, why are you asking me
all this if you can just read about it in the story? I
sought ---- out, okay? I knew ---- was somewhere on Gaia.

I knew because I was a part of this, you understand? I was written in! From the first I fell in ---- with ----, and I knew I would find ----. ---- was the key, don't you see? ---- was the ----ing orchestrator of this whole thing! I knew that I would steal the letters. That even though I didn't really believe what was going on, that it wasn't possible, I knew that even my doubts were part of the script. I knew I'd find ---- -- it wasn't like I didn't know where to look. It was right there in the letter! Actually, it's more accurate to say ---- found me, ---- brought me to ---- like a ----ing moth to the flame. ---- didn't give a ---- about me, of course. ---- only used me to get access to my mother, she's on the Council, you know that. She helped approve ----'s consultancy bid for the Eurydicette project. So ---- could get to the LHHK-000. Oh, ----, what's the use. Now you're gonna tell me to get off, that I'm crazy ... Look, I just want to be with ---- okay? That's all I want! I ---- ----! You ----! I ---- ----! I ---- ----!I ---- ----!

WITNESS REMOVED AND CITED WITH MULTIPLE LOGO INFRACTIONS AND LOGOCRIME. WITNESS TO BE YYY.6000, UU-09831, 870-IIOP AND KKL-0001 UNDER WWW457.PKI AND KEPT UNDER OBSERVATION AT

LEMURITE INSTITUTE IN NEW CHARLOTTE FOR THE AA.90-333, FOR

A PERIOD OF NO LESS THAN 91.25 LUNACYKES.

1157 0-DIRECTIVE   O-DIRECTIVE   O-DIRECTIVE O-DIRECTIVE

        O-DIRECTIVE   O-DIRECTIVE   O-DIRECTIVE O-DIRECTIVE

IN ACCORDANCE WITH EMERGENCY LEGISLATION 0-DIRECTIVE

9087345IE-RG8, SEC. 45757-575903I, PARAS. ORE09O0-97979-

.MMM-000, JJO-0098M, RERER-TY566, CHRONOCRIME CHARGE AND

ALL RELATED DISCOURSE REMOVED FROM RECORD, CHRONOCRIME

REMOVED FROM PENAL CODE STATUTES, CHRONOCRIME DECLARED

FICTIONAL MALAISE OF THE AA.90-333 PAGLIATED MIND OF GYN-

Y677T34 BY EMERGENCY LEGISLATION 9087345IERG845757575903-

IORE09O0-97979-.MMM-OOO. YOU HAVE BEEN INFORMED.

PROSECUTRIX TO CONVICT ACCUSED, PROVIDE CONCLUDING

SUMMATIONS AND CLOSE TRIAL.

PROSECUTRIX: Sisters, Gaia stands this day at a

crossroads, a true RTy77. We face anew the bald threat of

the Oppressor, risen like Sirena from the ashes of

herstory. From the first NC records, we know that our

sisters then, the first genizens, treasured, as do we now,

the freedoms bestowed upon our society through the noble

and ovarite sacrifices of the Martyrs and their founding of
the Matriarchate in lunacyke 0 NC. Every child from New
Atalanta to Europa-77 prime knows this story: how the
Oppressor fell from its age-old domination of the gyn race,
through its own scientific folly, how its reckless and
brutish experimentation with off-Gaia samples brought back
from Artemia reduced the XYs to brainless lumps, primitive
and incapable of thought, yet left the gyns -- heretofore
its slaves, the lowest of the low -- untouched, and as the
superior power obliged, decreed by blessed Luna, to rise up
and rebuild Gaia in a new image, our own image, to usher in
an unprecedented and glorious era of peace, prosperity,
scientific wonders and supreme ovocracy. We know all this,
young and old, and we have enjoyed the fruits of Gaia's
Womb for countless lunacykes.

Sisters, I turn to you now, I call on you to look about for
the cause of this alleged unrest. See before you these two
gyns, unbalanced and cowed by the monster XY-099, these two
noble gyns who thanks to our hallowed, gyneficent state
will receive treatment for this fiend's abuses, and be
restored to useful gynizenship. Understand, my sisters,
how easily the Matriarchate dispatches its enemies, how
readily we correct the negligible damage done by these

shadowy vestiges of XY Oppression, wherever and whenever they may appear. Have we not saved you? Have we not made life for each and every gyn the pinnacle of ontistence? Have we not streamlined the reproduction of our children to free up all our lives for the greater glory and use of the Matriarchate? Sisters, look about, I implore you. Look about for the roots of these vile rumors of a disturbance, a challenge to our great civilization, and you will see that it is once again the XY who is to blame. We shall deal with it, as we have dealt with every menace, every such retrograde manifestation, on and off-Gaia, to our way of life.

Sisters, be calm, I say. And ask yourselves: Have we not sheltered you? Have we not guarded you from every possible threat? Have we not rendered the surviving XY-099, brutish and pathetic specimens that they are, into servants for our purposes? Recall that every one of the XYs produced in the ovabanks, down to the last one in each solocyke quota, is automatically clystered into an XY-099. You know this. This rogue XY-099 is a fluke, an accident, nothing more. The monster is a freak, unique and unprecedented, there can be no others of its kind in store. If there were, they

would of course have no right to ontistence and be UYTYU- …
Yes, what is it?

**PROSECUTRIX AND ARBITRATIX CONFER IN PRIVATE.   SESSION
RECONVENCES AT 1147.**

REPORT CONCLUDES.

Sisters, the threat is allayed. The Matriarchate, through
its Hippocorps organ, has resolved the situation. We
pronounce the XY-099 guilty in absynthia – guilty of all
charges, guilty in triplicate irrevocably and forever, and
sentenced to the ultimate JJOL900, which sentence blessed
Luna has already seen fit to carry out. The convicted XY-
099 has been 309458klrtjfdlj, 39046oiretjkk0--0, and UYTYU-
866ed. You may now read the official herstory on your
linkmods. Luna be praised. Yes, the beast was successful,
distastefully as the thought may strike us, in producing an
XY through non-43085jfkdnLKH methods. The thing was
horribly deformed, an abomination. The unspeakable creature
was summarily UYTYU-866ed under code 985nbfldk-000, sec.
00900-pp, par. 55yi.

Be at ease, my sisters. As of 1200 all these disturbances

will cease, under DDD-Puoi9898-TXT. All rumors regarding

the proliferation of an XY-099 insurrection from the outer

colonies to Gaia and pertaining to an assault on the

capital, on this building, on this very hall from which

this linkcast emanates, my dear, dear sisters, shall be

severely XX-UYB97911-W. You have been informed. That is

all. The Prosecutrix rests. The stars and blessed Luna be

with us.

1203 O-DIRECTIVE O-DIRECTIVE O-DIRECTIVE O-DIRECTIVE

     O-DIRECTIVE O-DIRECTIVE O-DIRECTIVE O-DIRECTIVE

IN ACCORDANCE WITH EMERGENCY LEGISLATION O-DIRECTIVE

0986IORE-89658659859, SECT. 395736888-009UUT,

PAR.0990658887-OOP, ALL XY-O99S RE HEREBY DECLARED ILLEGAL

09857-CSA-44 AND SHALL PROCEED TO THE NEAREST D.I.S. CENTER

IN THEIR AREA FOR IMMEDIATE 908649-PPP-XYXY TREATMENT.

VIOLATORS TO BE 8869.XXV-7 ON SIGHT UNDER OVORITY OF

STATUTE 33-TRFF9, SEC. 66-ZZZ, PAR. 3. YOU HAVE BEEN

INFORMED. THE STARS AND BLESSED LUNA HERSELF BE WITH US.

1324 O-DIRECTIVE O-DIRECTIVE O-DIRECTIVE O-DIRECTIVE

O-DIRECTIVE O-DIRECTIVE O-DIRECTIVE O-DIRECTIVE

IN ACCORDANCE WITH EMERGENCY LEGISLATION O-DIRECTIVE 590-4368045UYIO0E-9YTIOR9989K, SECT. 2323EWWER56-QQQ, PARA. 990-ZZOOP-9900, THIS REPORT AND ALL REFERENCES TO "GENE NELSON" TO BE ZZZ.9900 FROM DATALINK IN THEIR ENTIRETY EFFECTIVE IMMEDIATELY, UNDER EMERGENCY OVORITY OF HIPPOCORPS HIGH COMMAND. EMERGENCY WAR PLAN LILITH PHASE I NOW IN EFFECT.

ALL MENTION OF "GENE NELSON," ON OR OFFLINK, THROUGHOUT THE MATRIARCHATE, TO BE XX.0988-I UNDER DDD-PUOI9898-TXT, PURSUANT TO ONTOCRIME STATUTES. VIOLATORS TO BE SENT TO SPECIAL 88-OPT-ATE-9997 FOR TREATMENT (ADDENDUM) OR 8869.XXV-7 ON SIGHT AT LOCAL HOPLICE DISCRETION. YOU HAVE BEEN INFORMED. THE STARS AND BLE

O-DIRECTIVE O-DIRECTIVE O-DIRECTIVE O-DIRECTIVE
O-DIRECTIVE O-DIRECTIVE O-DIRECTIVE O-DIRECTIVE

EMERGENCY WAR PLAN LILITH PHASE II NOW IN EFFECT. DEATH TO THE ENEMIES OF THE DAUGHTERS OF BLESSED LUNA.

INIATING UYTYU-866-D OF ALL DATA PERTAINING TO REPORT AND

CASE. THE STARS AND BLESSED LUNA BE WITH US.   SESSION

COMPLETE IN

5-NC,

4-NC,

3-NC,

2-NC,

THE STA

work obviously betrays a profound male castration

fear fraught with Lacanian mirror stage anxieties

of "clairvoyance envy" still all too typical in the

logophallocratic symbolic order. The "Letters'"

much-commented-on addendum, however, pertaining to

the future society of the gyns, represents another

level of intertexto-performo-neo-Kleinian phallo-

withering terror, and as such all womyn should

embrace its precepts. With its Other-empowering

vision of d[i]fferánce (in the Mihn-Hanian/

MacKinnonite unitarian project sense), with its

bold resolution of the I/i opposition into a

jouissance utopia, the addendum imbricates

"fantasy" with a positive *imago,* an Ovarian

intellectual riposte to the current NOTF lack-

driven dystopia, evidence for which can be seen in

the recent misogynistic "Mars '99" space mission to

"bring back" - onboard a titanium phallus, of

course, pap-smear-like soil samples and other rape

I draw the shade.

The birds are screaming their first, the East stirs the bare limnings of its inchoate, rosy nest.

But the dawn is deceived.

As I pry open its wrapping, the last text assaults my flaring nostrils with sulfur.

There are worlds within, voices babbling nowhere all together, all at once, a Dantean wet dream.   As unto them, I am everywhere, Pazuzu-like, I see it all, baby.

Out of the corner of one eye, in the window's reflection, stoked by the yellow glow of the table lamp beside me, I catch sight of myself as I read and reread.

Black, foul, eyes aflame in the pallid flicker of a computer screen, heavy-lidded, swallowed up in the endless tomb of my camera obscura, smelly ...

All this I see.

CEnTRAL MERiDIAN

And here gallop Picasso's bulls.
And here march Dali's elephants on spider's legs
And here rides the knight of La Mancha.
And here the Karamazovs carry Hamlet.
And here is the core of the atom.
And here is the cosmonaut's base on the moon.
And here stands a statue without its torch.
And here runs a torch without a statue.
And it's very simple: Where the man ends,
The flame begins.
And then in the silence can be heard the mumbling
of worms in the ashes. For
In essence billions of people
Are keeping silent.

> Miroslav Holub,
> *Jan Palach's Prague*

It was a pleasure to burn.

> Ray Bradbury,
> *Fahrenheit 451*

Wasn't ignoring you."

Strake says, "wouldnt want to interrupt your most intelligent conversation"

Funnyegyptncamel says, "ou peut etre pas ?11"

KATNIP LEAVES.

VALLEYGAY LEAVES, HEADED FOR PBD'S CHATHOUSE.

Tpbacano says, "yo tambien quiero papas fritas!!!!!"

QUEENEE ENTERS.

LIETUV ENTERS.

Rockinronnie says, "lopis where r u from"

Myjupiter says, "Nay!!! Como estas!?"

Creativehands says, "LOL toad >:-("

Giack says, "Ciao, qualche italiana?"

Radracer16 says, "20 minutes to reconnect"

SickofThis says, "Hey WEST you still there"

Catycalifornia says, "It anger my mother as well, she got spat on in the face by a black man for holding me. Go figure."

COKEGUY ENTERS.

Motie says, "SHHH, Snowy. Have Hearts fooled. :-D ;-) HHOS"

16J69 says, "Hello, SarahHeartburn. You have said you like art?"

Candy13 says, "No i don't have a boyfriend"

Nickelbag says, "real twist at the end, IMNSHO"

Lopiss says, "Puerto Rico."

DICKDRIP ENTERS.

DIXY-BOY ENTERS.

DIXY-BOY LEAVES, HEADED FOR UP-ALL-NIGHT CHAT ALLEY #4

SarahHeartburn says, "16J69, yes I do. I luv it. ;-)"

Emejiap says, "Hola Paho"

JEAN-LUCPICARD766 LEAVES.

Sufan says, "Youth is what you live it 8:-)"

Zwieback says, "anyone wanna talk with an eight-incher?"

Leebuchet says, "Stop reading Jos23 and communicate!!"

16J69 says, "SarahHeartburn, have you seen Central Meridian at the LACMA?"

NARIZON LEAVES.

Stargate692 says, "Do You Go To A Big School"

UP-ALL-NIGHT CHAT / AUG. 11, 1998

JOHNNY STORM LEAVES.

Leebuchet says, "From my friend in school, but I still need to practice more, Quecho."

Penetrator281 says, "That bathroom's a good country mile away."

Pullinghair says, ((((((((STEVE)))))))) @>--,--

DAENAA LEAVES, HEADED FOR UP-ALL-NIGHT COMPUTING.

FAMINE LEAVES, HEADED FOR UP-ALL-NIGHT STRIPTEASE DUNGEON.

SarahHeartburn says, "16J69, no I havent. Hungwell, just never you mind."

Steve88 says, "6 minutes to 11."

Torontotoad says, "I am totally with you, Ladyfreak! GMTA"

Nickelbag says, "My foul and malodorous spirit."

CABA says, "That's why they cremated Cobain"

Quecho says, "BAK"

Dickdrip says, "right, kafka. We are all beautiful in our way, people of all races don't have the understanding that we all really do need to get along. :'-)"

KAMALA LEAVES.

44D says, "sugarbear did you forget about me?"

KORKIE SMOOCHES STEVE88.

Jailbait says, "Dream on, Gabe"

Nickelbag says, "I'm not"

16J69 says, "I believe you would like it. Michael Milliken is the artist."

Hungwell says, "Same as the color timer."

Cokeguy says, "Well, Ladyfreak, I'm from Texas and people hate you out loud ... very loud!"

Penetrator578 says, "Thanks Ray."

Culero says, "ROFL "

PRAXIS ENTERS.

COKIEROBERTS LEAVES, HEADED FOR MASS ORGY ROOM #6.

Sufan says, "Johnny how old are you?"

Stargate692 says, "Do You Have Any Boy Friends"

Candy13 says, "8th"

IRON07 LEAVES.

UP-ALL-NIGHT CHAT / AUG. 11, 1998

Traveler43 says, "Bye Room Good Night :^)"
JACKMELOUD LEAVES, HEADED FOR SPORTSHOUSE #1.
Quecho says, "Where did you learn Spanish Lee?"
Sarahcan says, "Take care Traveler...."
Johnnyyuma1 says, "Too old I think, sometimes."
Mikko12 says, "Hi Iron!"
DICKDRIP LEAVES.
TRAVELER43 LEAVES, HEADED FOR CHAT ALLEY.
Quecho says, "De donde eres Emejiap?"
SarahHeartburn says, "Never heard of him. Where are you from?"
Grrila4 says, "Cobain who?"
Ladyfreak says, "Hey you all pass some Red Stripe."
Boromir says, "Suksuksuksusksuk"
WOOKIE73 LEAVES, HEADED FOR PRIVATE ROOM.
QUECHO says, "BTW does your name have a meaning lee?"
16J69 says, "I am Czech. A student of history at Charles
University in Prague."
SAMADAMS ENTERS.
STEVE88 LEAVES, HEADED FOR PRIVATE ROOM.
Superfox says, "you dumass."
PHIL-U-UP SMILES BECAUSE VAN HALEN IS ON.
Pullinghair says, "Cool avatar, lee"
Rudy II ENTERS.
Terrax5 says, "Sorry menn, no liquor in this house."
Paralon says, "Englehart was on there from about 230 on. Ben took
over the team."
Liverwort says, "Gimme head til I'm dead."
JasonIo says, "It's a useless precaution but absolutely
necessary."
SarahHeartburn says, "Oh, wow. I know tons of people who've gone
over there. Asia is real popular for tourists right now, right?
What's your name, 16J69?"
Lubyanka says, "Chevo ty menya osuzhdaesh, suka?"
LISAMARIE LEAVES, HEADED FOR UP-ALL-NIGHT HAPPY HOUR # 59.
LIETUV LEAVES.
Peace14 says, "do u ever come down this way"

UP-ALL-NIGHT CHAT / AUG. 11, 1998

WOMYN LEAVES, HEADED FOR SINGLES BAR #18.

Alliecat97 says, "how bout you stelbo"

Queerfucker says, ":-*"

Stelbo says, "hey peace 14 chat with me"

Affable says, "I just love your straight forward approach, you keep gaining marks!!! IMHO"

HOTRICH ENTERS.

16J69 says, "My name is Jan. I very much recommend this exhibit."

Peace14 says, "hello stelbo"

Jackme says, "how about me what :-ss)"

Candi21 says, "Honesty IS the best policy."

Nickelbag says, "consider the case closed."

Alliecat97 says, "what age are you"

Candi21 says, "Tell me about you."

MEZCLA LEAVES.

NUMBERR1GIRL ENTERS.

SNOOPDOGGITTY ENTERS.

SarahHeartburn says, "Exhibit? KrokerDoo, isn't it too hot in Texas for that?"

Excess says, "I have tried to figure, but it dosent add up!!"

Dickdrip says, "Nobody told me that fleas have knees."

Alliecat says, "I am a web mistress. :-)-8"

Bo&Peep12 says, "The needs of the many outweigh the needs of the few. Or the one."

CULERO LEAVES AND LOGS OFF.

16J69 says, "Central Meridian. It is an installation. I discovered it some weeks ago. SarahHeartburn, shall we go to a private room?"

Dryhump says, "M, tiembla y ve estrellas y fuegos artificiales y OVNIS y extraterrestres"

Ranxxeroxx says, "Coffee's burning."

KrokerDoo says, "Uh uh."

NACHOCHIP EMTERS.

Choad says, "44D where are u?"

Rudy II says, "Nobody told me that fleas eat cheese."

STARGATE LEAVES, HEADED FOR Q CONTINUEM #5.

UP-ALL-NIGHT CHAT / AUG. 11, 1998

CHATTERBOX ENTERS.

FREUDMOTHER ENTERS.

Dee-lite788 says, "Nichego podobnogo. Prosto xotel skazat, shto ty nepravilno vystupaesh s nyey."

SarahHeartburn says, "Sure. Zwieback, I'm going to ignore you if you don't stop that. just never you mind."

JESSICA5 says, "NO SHIT."

Freudmother says, "You are repeating yourself."

SarahHeartburn says, "Damn weirdos, everywhere."

Quecho says, "hijole, se va ha quemar el bato, que no, stelbo?"

Nickelbag, "Nejsem."

Lubyanka says, "Ponyal. Ty syuda v Albuquerque priezhayesh ne skoro?"

CREATIVEHANDS LEAVES, HEADED FOR NEWSROOM # 8.

16J69 says, "SarahHeartburn, shall we go to a private room so that we may speak more freely?"

Boromir says, "Suksusksusksusksusksusk"

CABA says, "just because you're paranoid C=}>;*{})"

T+ SWIRLS SNOWWHYTE AROUND ROOM, DANCING.

Dee-lite788 says, "Zhelatelno, snaesh? Ot deneg zavisit."

SarahHeartburn says, "Sure, 16J69. Too many sickos in this room."

LADYBEAR ENTERS.

ORPHYNYXX ENTERS.

Phil-u-up says, "last season sucked."

Nickelbag says, "want to be honest with you."

DoninTokyo says, "We have eaten the english salad."

Lietuv says, "Hey Jenny, C=}>;*{})."

Partyfreak10 says, "I'm a mother of two."

ENDOWED ENTERS THE ROOM.

POWDERFINGER LEAVES, HEADED FOR CHAT ALLEY.

Dulce says, "Strange fleas indeed"

LOHENGRIN ENTERS.

SPIRAL9 ENTERS.

SARAHHEARTBURN LEAVES, HEADED FOR PRIVATE ROOM.

Sufan says, "12 and a half."

UP-ALL-NIGHT CHAT / AUG. 11, 1998

Choad says, "divide it by the cosign and that should get it."

16J69 YOU HAVE LEFT CHATHOUSE ROMANCE, HEADED FOR PRIVATE ROOM.
16J69 YOU HAVE ENTERED PRIVATE ROOM.

16J69: SarahHeartburn, you are there?

SarahHeartburn: Sure, Jan. Hi.

16J69: Hello. Thank you for meeting me.

SarahHeartburn: Sure. You sound like a nice guy. My name is
Renée.

16J69: Very nice to meet you. What part of LA do you live in?

SarahHeartburn: Sorry, can't say. Let's keep this anonymous, OK?
Tell me about this installtion.

16J69: YEs. As i said, it is at LACMA. Milliken, is well-known
for his installations, I believe. He used to be a stage designer.
The exhibit depicts a garage, complete with car and many objects.
One may walk inside.

SarahHeartburn: Wow. I don't know that much about installations.
It sounds way cool. I haven't heard M.'s name before, in art
world or stage world. But never you mind.

16J69: Do you know stage world?

SarahHeartburn: I'm an actress.

16J69: That is interesting. What kind of action do you do?

SarahHeartburn: Everything: movies, commercials, TV, theater.
Whatever my agent can get. You might have seen me. I model some
too.

16J69: I have gone a number of times to our theatre in Prague. It
is called Narodni divadlo. "National Theatre." People come from
the provinces to see inexpensive shows. It is a very famous
theatre, established in 1863. Where do you act.

SarahHeartburn: It always depends. You know, you take what you ca
get. My agent says I'm doing pretty well. I'm 22, so I should do
OK for a few more years, haha.:->

16J69: That is wonderful. Theatre is very important. Have you
heard of the theatre Polanski's Puppets on 51st street?

UP-ALL-NIGHT CHAT / AUG. 11, 1998

SarahHeartburn: No. Your English is good. How old are you?

16J69: I am 20. Today, in fact, is my birthday

SarahHeartburn: Oh, wow! Happy Brithday!

16J69: Thank you.

SarahHeartburn: What are you gonna do?

16J69: It is late already. But I spent the day with my mother and brother Jiri and my friend Helen. We are from a small town near Prague, Vsetaty.

SarahHeartburn: Wow. Are they all here with you in LA?

16J69: Yes.

SarahHeartburn: Cool. My parents are in Scotland.

16J69: You are Scottish?

SarahHeartburn: Half. I have very red hair. My dad is from there. I have duel citizenship.

16J69: Do you go to chat houses often?

SarahHeartburn: Once in a while, if I have time. Its fun. But sometimes the sickos get to be a pain.

16J69: Do they really bother you?

SarahHeartburn: Oh, yeah. Like, right now, that zwieback. He was PMing me, saying all these sick things. Forget it. Jan, I HOPE YOUR NOT A SICKO.

16J69: I am not certain what you mean. but I think, no.

SarahHeartburn: Good.

16J69: I am not sure this word sicko. We are all human beings, however we may be different. We are all placed here to help each other, no? we are all comrades. So i believe.

SarahHeartburn: Thats sweet. Hay, I would liek to see this exhibit. Central Mediterranen.

16J69: Central Meridian. Shall we meet? I can show it to you. the museumis on Wilshire street.

UP-ALL-NIGHT CHAT / AUG. 11, 1998

SarahHeartburn: No, Jan. I think we should keep this anonmous.

16J69: You sound like a nice person.

SarahHeartburn: You too. But promise me you won't ask to meet me, OK? I've had some bad experiences on the net.

16J69: I am sorry to hear that. what kind expereinces?

SarahHeartburn: Better not say. I have no time for a boyfriend. Let's be net friends, OK?

16J69: Yes.

SarahHeartburn: Jan is a funny name.

16J69: There are many Jans in Czech history. It is like your John or Juan or Ian. My father loved our great figures from our past: Jan Hus, Jan Komensky, Jan Zizka, Jan Zimmer, Jan Neruda, Jan Opletal. He named me for them.

SarahHeartburn: Thats sweet. What about Jan Michael Vincent? LOL

16J69: I do not knnow him.

SarahHeartburn: Just kidding.

16J69: Most people say I am a serious person.

SarahHeartburn: But you like art. Can't study all the time.

16J69: I must make my family and country proud for me, especially now. at this time. It is too bad we cannot meet, Renee. We both live here.

SarahHeartburn: Sorry Jan. No can do. But I pomise I'll see the exhibit.

16J69: You seem very nice.

SarahHeartburn: You too. Do you have many friends in LA?

16J69: Yes. Pavel, Ladislav, Eva, Helen. also fro university. Will you give me your number please, or e-mail?

SarahHeartburn: Jan, i said no. No meeting. No flesh. If I gave you my e-mail you caould find me. You could be a real sickie.

16J69: I am sorry. I will not ask again.

SarahHeartburn: OK. Thank you. :)

UP-ALL-NIGHT CHAT / AUG. 11, 1998

16J69: I do get somewhat lonesome. It is a rather sad time for me. for my country. sometimes it is hard. I am not always best student.

SarahHeartburn: I'll tell you what, Jan. I won't meet you, but we can write each otherin the little book inside the museum.

16J69: I do not understand.

SarahHeartburn: The little book, inside the hall there? Do you know it?

16J69: inside the museum hall?

SarahHeartburn: right. the little book there.

16J69: Yes. You have been to the museum before?

SarahHeartburn: I've lived in LA for ten years. Sure I've been to LACMA. What floor is the inst. in?

16J69: 2. The Armand Hammer building.

SarahHeartburn: Does that floor have a little book? You knw, for. everybody to write in?

16J69: I believe so. Milliken has his own booklet just for C.M.

SarahHeartburn: Perfect. An ex-boyfriend and I used to leave little "secret messages" to each other there. Two years ago. It was cute and fun. He was an artist. I'll drop you a line there sometime this week. I think I have some time before a shoot I am doing.

16J69: Are you certain?

SarahHeartburn: Sure I'm sure. It will be fun. But promise me PROMISE me that you WILL NOT try to meet me. I'm going to trust you, Jan. My dad says I should n't do thing slike this in this city, but I'm going to trust you.

16J69: Thank you. I promise. I give you my word.

SarahHeartburn: Thank you. TTFN, Jan. gotta go.

16J69: You will write something thi week? It's good because I will go again. I go often, Milliken changes the exhibit often. He has a gorilla inside the garage that he moves

SarahHeartburn: You can write me about it OK? Gotta go now.

UP-ALL-NIGHT CHAT / AUG. 11, 1998

expecting a call.   :-*

16J69: Yes.   Thank you.   I will await your message. I think you
will like it.   Renee, what does symbol :-* mean?

SarahHeartburn: It means a kiss, Jan.

SARAHHEARTBURN HAS LEFT PRIVATE ROOM, HEADED FOR CHAT ALLEY
SARAHHEARTBURN IS NO LONGER LOGGED ON TO UP-ALL-NIGHT CHAT

16J69 YOU HAVE LEFT PRIVATE ROOM, HEADED FOR CHAT ALLEY
16J69 YOU ARE NO LONGER LOGGED ON TO UP-ALL-NIGHT CHAT
        SEE YOU SOON!

UP-ALL-NIGHT CHAT / AUG. 11, 1998

exactly sixteen years ago, but now you could sit by the freeway all day long and never catch sight of one. It's the tires. White wall, Bortel 1As. Man, I wish I'd never given that thing away to my cousin. He wrecked it inside of three months. Anyway, thanks again for the memorys.

> Chuck Hale, Portsmouth, VA
> and family

Enchanting. Delightful. Very L.A. Why the name? We still have concerns of that. Just wondering indifferently. We will return again.
> Masha Vinograd, Omsk, RU

Esta era mi septima ves. Eres un genio. Casate con migo, te lo ruego, no lo

Lovely! The whole inside of the garage made me all spooky, all heebee-jeebee. Please don't ever leave, because my cousin Marge from Fargo has just got to see this, oh, please make this a permanent I think they're getting wise to us. Today Miss Jean Brodie gave me the evil eye the whole time I was walking around the Chagalls, staring at me like a hawk. then when I come out of the powder room to get a drink, she walks up to me and doesnt even let me get up from the fountain and she says, (something like,) "I think you need to check that purse in," — but she's let me carry it in and out of here for weeks! She just had this look in her eye.   I wish I knew Latin or something or hay, how about Czech so that I wouldn't feel this like paranoia about her reading this. I hope you're around, Jan. be careful. She's always creeping around the corner. I'll probably come in again on Tuesday. Audition tomorrow. Hope you're feeling better. Renée PS. There's a pigeon skull lodged inside one of the doll arms, by the first screen door. I climbed up on the newspapers real quick and got a look. Kunta Kintei didn't see me. Lovely! Lovely! I can't thank you enough! God bless you, Mr. Milliken, sir!

> Luca Luciano,
> Fastville, Ohio

Que cosas tienen. Se parece al lugar donde trabajo. Si quieres ven, te lo enseño. Muy agradecido.

> Manuel Farrias, Fresno

I think this is neat. Age 5. Name: Miyoshi.

My only problem with it, personally, is all the junk. I take this meditation class once a week and the first thing they tell you: throw all that shit out. Its clutter, clutters your lungs, clutters your soul, your mind. Take out those newspapers (they look like stuff someone left up in their attic), those tires, typewriters, mood rings, receipts, etc. (you know what I mean) — take it out and burn it, or sell it. Theirs this huge dumpster right near Salinas, nobody ever goes down there. You take Highway 101 north and just passed the town, their it is. I live right by it. I'll help. I really think

September 30, 1998

Det eneste "ægyptiske" ved det er sandet på gulvet. Hvor flad, trist, udtrådt og ugivtig den udstilling forekommer mig!

Amled Sloth,
Helsingør, Danmark

Ah, a breath of fresh air. Installation meets Hollywood set. Am I right? Yes I am.

Molly Molt, Silverlake

Rosebud
Rosebud
RosebudRosebudRosebudRosebudRosebudRosebudRosebudRosebudRosebudRosebudRosebud
RosebudRosebudRosebudRosebudRosebudRosebudRosebudRosebudRosebudRosebudRosebud
Rosebud
Rosebud?

Whoa! Y'all get all kinds here, huh? I guess eveybody passes through here at one time or another, a big place like this an' all, the weirdos too. We saw us a couple just now. For what it's worth, me and the wife had a holler. That's my two cents. Good show. we wish you luck and success in your future endeavours.

Yes, sir. Very nice. Very profund. What he said.

Jake & Mindy Slate, Midland, TX

My quest is over. I have found the answer. This work, this work is God. You are God. God is Californian. God lives in Santa Monica. God is thank you for the tip. Yes, I am feeling better. I get, as you say, a little "hot under the collar" sometimes. Yes, I saw the stuffed bird. But did you notice the gorilla, which is now behind Saturn? And that Pluto has a new moon, Charon? The boatman, the river Styx. Ferryman of the dead. Today is Wednesday, you see, R. He has begun to come in on Wednesdays. Other new discoveries: a tiny smashed butterfly (mnymosene mnymosene? I believe so) dangling from inside the radiator grill; two new freckles on the dummy (left cheek); the north-northwest shopping list now demands <u>three</u> packs of carrots. Still feel odd when I read those recent restaurant receipts. There is one from September 12! O'Brien's diner! What troubles me is the music, the third number, after the (exactly!) seven minutes of static. A woman's voice, scratched. An opera? I do not know. I know little of music. Help, please! Hope you are now taking my advice to save these letters. Jan PS. You should not call him Kunta. I am serious. We must respect all nations, races, luck, fortune, chance, aleotary life, thrown to the winds, my savior, my liberator from Elysium! The gates are open, the Heaven light revealed! Kiss my burning cheek with your lips of thorns, your nimbic astigmatism, I am your yours, I rise on daggers of light.

Sincerely,
Antoinette Cormorant
Llano, NM

这是我看过的最悲哀的东西。谢谢你的诚实。　　王曼华

168

October 3, 1998

Un uomo di colore molto maleducato - penso fosse americano - non ci ha lasciato guardare dentro il laboratorio, a me e a mio fratello. Se ne è rimasto là come uno stupido, sbarrandoci l'entrata. Abbiamo potuto ascoltare solo la musica. Vorremmo lamentarci di persona, ma non parliamo bene l'inglese.

Mario Bellini,
Venezia, Italia

Niemals zuvor sind durch ein Kunstwerk solche Gefühle und Ängste in mir hervogerufe worden.

Me and the Mrs. here was pleased as punch to take part in this here voyage a discovery, cuz back home our system seems to be working really well. Miss Jean Brodie has to cover the whole wing, so she's usually gone for as long as fifteen minutes. Plenty of time to rip out your note, write mine and walk away. Yes, yes, I started saving them. It's like being a spy!! Kunta Kintey fell alseep again today! Oh, sorry. the "African-American staff member." Is everybody so PC in Prague? LOL The music is Mary Garden singing Claude Debussey's (SP.?) "Mes longs cheveux," (SP??) from a (very) rare wax recording made in 1904. Who knows how the hell Milliken found it. My friend Clarissa, who teaches Music at Stanford, gave me the scoop. I taped the radio and played it for her over the phone. That's cheating, I know. Well, girls can cheat! Like I really have time to look things up anyway. Lunches, lunches, agents, contacts. I must kill and eat your children. Ciao! Renée. PS. Oh, my god — M.J.B. has a HUGE run in her hose today. Left leg, near the ankle! for us to think about once we make it back to ole Missoula. Thanke kindly.

Luke Sargent
Missoula, Florida

I feel the identifying cards for the exhibit should be larger. It is hard for older visitors to read and walk through here. Thanks.

Keiko Ishigami
Garden Gate, OH

Wonderful museum! Please keep it open.
Bettie D. Paffe, Islington, VT

October 4, 1998

We find the exhibit somewhat inappropriate for children. Why all these corporate labels? All this jetsam of capitalism? Nissan vacuum control tubes, Ken Harvey's chassis parts, Castrol lubricant cans, Glowing Star detergent my congratulations on finding the music. He has kept it constant for months. As of now I have identifeid the three pieces: Ralph Burns' "Sprang" (recorded Feb 4, 1955); a bergamasca used by Girolamo Frescobaldi in Fiori Musicali (1635); and now the Mary Garden. Excellent! Thank you for saving our correspondence. "The lightest ink is sharper than the sharpest memory," as the Chinese say. Ace acrylic semi-gloss latex foam caps, Rand McNally road maps, El Cerrito restaurant calendar from 1949, Hastings air conditioner filters, and the list goes on. Does Mr. Milliken have no shame or concern for the young, that he has corporate sponsorship maquerading as art?

Sincerely,
Jerry Sin Chiang
Detroit, MI

樋口健次 :

見るとデイズニーランドを思い出した。特にあのゴリラが。でもさ、他人の男がちょっど僕の前に立っちゃって、実験室の中が全然見えなくなちゃった。それに、動いてくれないし。あの人、ただボーッとそこにつ立っていたよね。何か文句を言いたかったけれど、お母さんはそっとしておきなさいって。他のお客さんも見たいことぐらい誰でも知っているはずなのに。。。

The green Dart is a great touch. What is it about that model that holds such a fascination for us as a culture? Things have quieted down a bit in the capital. There are threats of strikes in the student union. I stand firm with my fellows. 1939 must never happen again and I don't think it will. We won't left you something inside TV under skeleton's right leg J. with Tucker upholstery, and who knows how many of us were conceived in these things, like in that Keinholz you've got in the hall. Great job and keep on truckin'!

Rufus Wallace
La Jolla, CA

ПИЗДОЙ МЕЛЬКНУТЬ, ЖИДОВКА!   НЕ ХУЙ,
ПИЗДА КОБЫЛЯ МНЕ НРАВИТСЯ   ВАСЯ!

Brilliant, except for the fumes. Do you actually run that car?

Liz Ramirez, Jacksonville, FL

Blahopřeju! Dokonale·jste vystihl atmosféru egyptské hrobky. Jsem egyptolog z
Olomouce a přijel jsem, protože jsem četl o vaší práci v novinách. Jsem rád, že
jsem přijel. Ale musím říct, že gorily v zemi faraonů původně nežily!

Vladimír Houšek

The museums's nice. The exhibit is nice. The people the staff, are real nice. Sorry I
haven't been in in a while. Long night last night. Producer's party, people getting
dunked in the pool. Hellacious head-splitter. Oh, you know what? Today I saw
him. Milliken! He's not white-haired at all, like I imagined. A little bald guy, late
forties. I told him I loved it and he said something about installations, the
"blending of space," Egypt, etc. He wouldn't tell me where he put the gorilla. R. PS.
I got your "present" out of the TV just in time. M. was digging around in there just
minutes after me. Be careful! We're gonna get in trouble. M.J. Brodie's suspicious,
I know it. Why did you want me to have this for anyway? Why did you save and
print out how we met? Jan, I said I wanted no weird stuff nice is just the best way to
describe it. So, so nice. Please don't lose your niceness.

Emma Winestock
Lichen, OR

Ich fand es anmaßend und unoriginell.

In Deutschland haben wir "Installations-Kunst"

seit dem Krieg. Dieses theoretische Grübeln

~~zielen auf~~ ist Selbstverliebtheit und läßt den Betrachter kalt.

Verschwende meine Zeit nicht damit! Außerdem, ein

Schwarzer, der schlecht roch, hat mich dauernd

angerempelt. Viel Glück!

I know I will return to see this again. I was stunned. I thought I had seen it all. But
once I penetrated the outer screen door (I had passed it by the first time, thinking it
was an actual part of the building!), it was like an epiphany. I spent over two hours
in there. I dragged my best friend, on the way telling him, "This is the closest thing
to a holodeck you and I are ever going to get." Inside again, I was rapturous.
"We've penetrated the art space!" I kept repeating. "We're there!" Mr. Milliken,
you've done what I thought an impossibility. You've actually given me a reason to
come to LA. I'm buzzing. I'm on fucking fire. Who knows, I might even write a

October 14, 1998

When I was growing up in south Indiana (right outside Bloomington), my best friend and I would play pirates and Civil War in my dad's work shed. It was huge. He used it to store our boat there, and to do woodwork. He would only be there on Saturdays in the summer, so my friend Jerrod and I had all Sunday afternoon after church to play in it. We couldn't wait to get home and take off our Sunday clothes so we could get all dirty and happy again in the shed. That shed had everything you can imagine. A big antique Hildegard buzzsaw, six or seven old fans (including a rusty ceiling fan from before the war, I think), spare parts, even an old abacus from Russia. For us that shed was like the whole world inside four walls. Our cat Jessie had three litters in one corner, right next to an old lawn mover, three years in a row. In the summers it was the best place to escape the burning heat, cool shade, spiderwebs, wooden swords we'd made ourselves. The boat was the Santa Maria, I was Columbus. Jerrod was an Indian. You could just sit there, all sweaty and tired after playing and look out the door or the window at the pond we had, and squeeze your eyes to make the glints on the water more geometrical, more like real triangles. Just when we needed her, Mom would come in from the house with a tray of lemonade and cucumber sandwiches, cut up in little squares. God, that was the best. Mom died two years ago, but that's the way I'll always remember her, smiling in her apron, there in the bright doorway, her hair still all done up after church, bringing me and Jerrod our lunch. "Don't go using my tray for a pirate shield, now," she would say. Every year I go back home to visit Pop, and by God, that shed's still there. The boat's gone (or rotted down into the ground, who knows?), but Dad still putters around in the shed with his cabinets and bed posts and bird houses. The pond's dried up, Jerrod's somewhere in Europe, but the same spider webs, the same rusty junk's still there, waiting, the same cracked mirror lying on the dusty plastic blue kid's swimming pool, that hasn't tasted water in 20 years. Everytime I see it I almost expect Jessie to jump out from behind it and meow hello. I humbly thank you, Mr. Milliken. I thank from the bottom of my heart for taking me back to my father's shed without even having to leave the city. With affection,

Arnold Wang, Woodland Hills

Lisa Ramone Indulge and you bulge! 8 ears old.

I counted 85 spaces in the parking garage. One of them should be given to the Dart. It's perfectly good! And what's more did you read the passage by the man from Indiana? It reminded me of my own father. He was not exactly a carpenter or inventor, but he was very good at his trade: confection. We had our own confectionery and sweets shop in Všetaty, before it was closed down. My father died when I was 13, of a heart attack. Probably the thing that's scarred most deeply onto my memory is the day of his cremation, the coffin, all black, with flowers on top. I felt sad they would burn my papa, but even then I realized, deep inside, that it was for the best. The purity of the flames was the best treatment for my poor father's body. The Hindus believe that cremation releases their dead from the putrefaction of flesh, burns away the pollutions of the body, of sin itself, transforms them into the spiritual incorruptibility of ash. In the Vedic patheon, all sacrifices to the deities must go through the fire god Agni, the cleanser. Secretly I felt this, I think, and knew my father was well-served. J. because with new paint job and if you took that scary dummy out of the front seat, it would work just fine. LA needs more cars, sir.

Alfred Lustig
Echo Park
213-555-0863

Det eneste "ægyptiske" ved det er sandet på gulvet. Hvor flad, trist, udtrådt og ugivtig den udstilling forekommer mig!

Amled Sloth, Helsingør, Danmark

Ho dovuto trascinarci il mio ragazzo, ma ne è valsa la pena. Nonostante le sue risate sguaiate e il suo sarcasmo, penso che gli sia proprio piaciuto. Abbiamo provato entrambi uno strano senso di deja vu, di riconoscimento, difficile da identificare. Ma escludo di aver visto niente del genere prima. Io è la prima volta che vengo a Los Angeles e il mio ragazzo non è tipo da andare per musei da solo. Molto interessante. In genere, preferisco la pittura alla moderna Environment Art, ma questo è stato qualcosa di speciale. Si ha l'impressione di innamorarsi delle cose, dell'effluvio degli oggetti. Ho percepito una santità, una sacrosanta predisposizione alla venerazione, prima ancora di leggere la spiegazione e l'affermazione dell'artista. La cosa che non mi aspettavo è il suo soffermarsi sulla morte. Non mi sento a mio agio a discutere di morte, o anche solo a pensarci, forse perchè sono donna. Certo, mi rendo conto che tutto ciò è naturale, che tutti noi possiamo morire persino molte volte per poi ritornare, ogni volta con una nuova identità. Tutto questo mi appare chiaro e comprensibile. Eppure questo pensiero continua a riempirmi di terrore; è per questo che ho preferito minimizzare quella parte del suo lavoro per godermi invece la meravigliosa e tenera evocazione della vita che rappresenta. Questo garage, pieno di cose morte, risplende del bagliore della vita. Sotto la polvere e le ragnatele, questi oggett sorridono. Spero di poter discutere a lungo di questo con il mio ragazzo, sia qui che una volta di ritorno a San Francisco. Mi piacerebbe ritornare e avere più tempo per vedere le molte cose che ancora non ho visto, ma lui deve ritornare al suo lavoro in ospedale. Grazie per quest'opera toccante e profonda, e buona fortuna per il futuro.

Tonya Bartoli, Milano, Italia

PS. spaghetti cappucino R. gorilla under Neptune look in mouthJ. linguini Corleone pizza fettucine a long time to come.

And, finally, still running at the Los Angeles County Museum of Art is *Central Meridian,* Michael Milliken's "permanent" installation tribute to American junk culture. In this delightful mixed-media re-creation of some fictional mad scientist's bungalow circa 19??, the Santa Monica artist weaves a colorful tapestry of diverse objects salvaged from garbage dumps, friends' attics and flea markets into a crazy, multifarious symphony cacophonous enough to mix many a reviewer's metaphors.

What looks like a large shed taking up most of LACMA's Burt Ward Hall (with a baby carriage on the tin roof, natch) opens up via an ordinary screen door upon a dark world of rusty, dusty, crusty splendor. A tool room packed full of every imaginable garden instrument first greets the visitor. Newspapers lie about in tied-together bundles, cobwebs dangle from the corners, and it's wall to wall shovels, buckets, hammers, washcloths, garden hoses, picture frames, lawn mowers, weed-eaters and all the other indescribable flotsam and jetsam that you've seen a thousand times in such places, all those knickknacks that cling like refrigerator magnets to the fat, well-pleased underbelly of the American dream. But in this most familiar, most banal of all settings, you need only look up to feel a disturbing unease — a not-quite-rightness. Doll parts hang down from the rafters, little decapitated toddler heads, arms, buttocks, while, swinging among them: small aluminum balls on string labeled "Pluto" and "Neptune." Curiouser and curiouser.

Another creaking screen door leads to the main chamber: a trashy, lived-in, authentic-smelling garage with oil stains on the floor; city ordinances and TEMPORARILY OUT OF GAS signs on the walls; a dusty counter top with pens, clips, towels, scraps of Rio Suite Hotel and Casino stationery, Astro Galaxy firecracker wrappers, Japanese postage stamps, etc., etc., and everywhere else: old klieglights, Walk-a-Pon liquid vinyl floor coating cans, rusty license plates, coat hangers, mounted deer, caribou and fox heads, baseball trophies, Folger's, Maxwell House, Butter-Nut, Yuba and Sandra coffee tins, six and half pairs of beat-up old skis (hanging), a faded print of a 17th-century German cartoon, restaurant receipts, fortune cookie slips ("Don't look back, always ahead"), tire jacks, Witteleind patching plaster boxes, toy trucks, amputated bike handlebars, a tattered lab coat, little dangling alluminum Uranus, Jupiter, Saturn, Mars, Earth, Mercury (no Venus?), newspapers, newspapers, newspapers, Stop 'n' Go cups, a Bee-Gee's concert poster, an eye chart, cereal boxes, chopsticks, watering cans, roller paint brushes and still more countless minutia, more, more ... more stuff. Lots more. Folded wheelchairs, wound sleeping cables, mops, trashcans, dead typewriters, pushpins, wrenches,

mattress springs, water-bobbing
plastic roadrunners, Elvis mugs,
central heating filters, baseball
caps, greasy rags, and still, more
more more: every conceivable thing
that you could picture coming down a
conveyor belt, getting packed up in
plastic and being shipped off to the
waiting masses.

Presiding over it all like a metal
and glass ziggurat is the room's
crowning glory, the towering sun that
holds the shiny wrinkled planets in
its grip, that sits on its plinth with
the stateliness of a dead Chinese
emperor: a green, 1964 Dodge Dart. I
could tell you about the little
laboratory (with its creepy radio)
attached to the side (its bizarre
bric-a-brac heightens the unheimlich
"mad scientist" motif); or I could
describe the ancient Sylvania TV set
with a baby skeleton in its hollow
innards; or point out the beach wave
sounds that emanate from behind the
garage's large wooden doors, leading
perhaps to some unseen tropical
paradise; or even try, just try, to
give you a sense of the utter
weirdness involved in looking inside
the Dart's passenger window and having
a wide-grinned Howdy Doody stare back
at you from the driver's seat, one
waxy hand on the wheel. I could, as
well, I suppose, launch into a
discussion of the artist's purported
goal with this project: to marry
American cast-off-and-bauble culture
with ancient Egyptian tomb design —
and all the rich readings *that*

provides.

But words, gentle reader, — not to
mention available column inches — can
only do so much. Suffice it to say
that Milliken is a master of the
double-take, a witty and disconcerting
mad-hatter who invites his glazed-eyed
guests to rummage, explore, bend down,
strain up, peep in and out of all the
nooks and shadows, to always find
there the unexpected, the outrageous,
and, often, the nightmarish.

Central Meridian is a magnificent
follow-up to Milliken's previous
installation *Pavilion of Rain* (which
ran at the Oakland Art Museum in
1993), a similarly junky cabin
complete with miniature pond and real
summer torrents every twenty minutes.
Moreover, I would be remiss in my LA
journalist duties if I didn't mention
that Milliken has a background in film
and stage design, (he worked on such
sci-fi classics as *Go Forth and
Replicate* and *Loving the Alien*) and it
is this experience, this attention to
the minutest details of reality-
mimicking sets that bring *Central
Meridian's* thousands of dead objects
to stunning, humming, irrefragable
life. Why, it's almost too real. You
schizophrenics, don't forget your
dopamine.

Ah, I almost forgot. The gorilla.
Can't forget the gorilla. Milliken,
who considers *CM* a work in progress,
slips a gorilla, in different guises,
into various secret hiding places
throughout the garage, moving it
around once a week. This has turned

the artist's growing legions of
devoted fans (a minor LA subculture in
its own right) into avid "monkey
hunters." But enough. Tourists,
friends, Romans, Egyptologists,
clutter-freaks, get thee to *Central
Meridian* mach schnell. In Milliken's
"post-human" Ameritrashscapes, the
only thing missing is people. That's
where you come in. Darn it, this
isn't "junk!" This is ART, folks,
ART!   Rob-O says check it out.

LACMA *is located at 2151 Wilshire
Boulevard, tel. 213-555-9087. Closed
Mondays.*

Artists, or what passes for them these days, seem more concerned with posing questions than providing answers. Irresolution is the flavor of the month. Ha! Of the decade. Now jumping onto the crowded confines of this trendy bandwagon is Michael Milliken, an "installationer," heir to Edward Keinholz and his 60s ilk — the generation most responsible for turning a once-bright art form into cheap, kitschy commerce. And so, Mr. Milliken will doubtless find plenty of gaga-eyed suckers eager to pay LACMA's stiff entry fee to see his latest glorified little play set, *Central Meridian.*

If this messy mixed-media monstrosity proves anything, it's that Hollywood connections (Milliken's father worked in the film industry and the artist himself seems to have spent too much time on the set of *Taxi)* will get you whatever you want in this art scene.

I won't tire you with details. All you need remember is Milliken's previous disaster, the odious and obnoxious *Pavilion of Rain,* a literal wet dream of the artist's to spray water on his audience at 20-minute intervals while boring them with faux Hawaiian settings lifted from *McHale's Navy.*

Not surprisingly, *Central Meridian* (yet another oh-so-suggestive, empty title) proves to be no less pretentious. Call me a cold, stuffed-crotch fishwife (and believe me, some have) but it just burns me up to see talentless set-dressers like Milliken parading around the city, proclaiming grand new theories of "total environment" and "ruptured space." The only thing total is this artist's wasting of my time, the only thing "ruptured" is my patience. Mr. Milliken, like my ex-husband, is a deluded hack full of pathetic ideas he'd be better off keeping between himself and his favorite white-streaked blanket, not spewing them on his audience like a pill-popping Walt Disney wannabe.

As for *Central Meridian,* I need point the reader's attention no further than the rusty baby carriage which "adorns" the "work's" smeared exterior, sitting on its roof like some heroin-induced melding of Eisenstein and Tennessee Williams. This blatantly anti-woman image is reason enough to walk on, and maybe give Keinholz's stomach-turning *Back Seat Dodge '38,* which contaminates the adjacent hall, a nice round kick for good measure.

Pitiful as it may seem, it's come to my attention that a loose "club" of Milliken groupies has hit on the idea of exploring *Central Meridian,* like grubs burrowing into a dead rabid dog. They spend hours a day inside the garage, which is modeled after an Egyptian tomb (oh, please Mr. Milliken, you're so clever, so cultured, so ethnically aware, take me now, now, Mr. Milliken, inside the Dart), seeking out its hidden "clues." Their shaggy grail: a protean gorilla that hides out in different locations, presumably eating its own excrement in obscurity while it waits to be discovered. If only its creator would do the same. Alas, Milliken continues to "tinker" with the work to this day, milking his LACMA meal ticket of ever more resources better spent on real artists. The ever-changing tableaux (if we can call moving bits of junk and a gorilla around once a week "tableaux") has inspired quite a following of odd but committed morons with too much time on their hands. Just more self-abusing "artistic" irresolution — the the toast of the century. Just another way, I suppose, to distract yourself from real life in this howling, f—ing city.

— Elda Comintas

October 16, 1998

Sound of audio in installation VERY instrusive — Janice Riddle Rundberg, NV

Nevím proč, ale výstava mě rozrušila a rozesmutnila. Je těžké říct, co presně mi
nesedí. Vaše práce je krásná, mocné, dívala jsem se na ni dlouho, de'le než hodinu.
Dojalo mě to. Ty předměty, ticho, klid, tma — padlo to na mě a začala jsem plakat.
Vzpomněla jsem si na svého bratra Jana, který se utopil před dvěma roky. Vždycky
se chtěl podívat do Ameriky. Připomněl jste mi jeho smrt, hluboko zasutou v srdci.
Nikdy jsem o tom s nikým nemluvila. Byli jsme si velice blízcí. Pak jsem ho
najednou uviděla, jak tam stojí u kalendáře — mladý muž, co vypadal tolik jako
můj bratr, že jsem se zajíkla a rychle odešla z haly. Manžel a dcera přišli za mnou —
co se stalo. Nic jsem jim neřekla. Mrzí mě, že se nedokážu dobře vyjádřit, chybí mi
slova.

Hanka Moravcová
Karlovy Vary, CS

我夫人看了一直在笑："看这些植物！看这些大猩猩！" 我们是从
台北来的。我们特别喜欢这个展览。我们的小男孩一直想爬
进汽车里去。小孩子说："爸爸！这里面有个死人！" 他看见的
时候很害怕。也许你应该把死人搬走。它会吓着小孩的。除
此之外，我们非常喜欢你的作品。谢谢。

王 梅林

Fantastisk. Hvad det så end betyder.
Kim Petersen, Vejle, Danmark

Kinda hokey. What's the big deal? People around me, all these furners oohing and
ahing. It's just a damn garage. Come over to my place if you want Jan, stop leaving
me things in the exhibit! I can't guarantee that I'll come on the days when I say, and
we're going to get caught one of these days. They're even writing about us in the
media. What's the matter with you? I'm going to stop this if you don't quit! R. PS.
It was a pretty funny article, though. Sorry to lose my cool. Nervous about my
audition on Monday after eight or nine days living with me you won't want to see
no goddamm garage agin!

Johnny Rotten Lucre, Delaware

October 20, 1998

Things, things, things. Often they are all that we leave behind, or that is left to us. Americans think of themselves as recyclers, as materialists. But you are in fact only disposers. What is on all the shelves one year you will find in the city dumps the next. In Czechoslovakia we have been the true "environmentalists" for centuries, since before the Hapsburg yoke. My mother keeps the salt in an old Aspirin jar, never thrown away. My father has used the same pipe for 20 years, though I hate it when he smokes. As Milleken says in his statement: "There's something about the poetry of junk. It's corny, but this is part of the wheel of life. We leave ourselves in these objects, and when we're gone we're still there, lingering inside them." I love these objects as I love my mother's scratched-up Aspirin jar.

Pavel Stransky
Vienna

We like America. We like come to America look at big buildings with lights and movie stars. LA! Swmimming pools! We like all I can say is I wish I could "dispose" of my car. A '96 Celica. God, the thing's ready to fall apart. I know, I know, this nut up here's probably going to tell me they hold on to their cars for 50 years in his country, but in LA that wouldn't fly. Not for everybody I know, anyway. Anyway, I'm doing a commercial the next few days so I'll probably get back here next week. Some European perfume. Money's good. Hope you're doing okay. You've never missed a day before. R. P.S. I counted eight new freckles on the dummy. And 57 different pens on the garage counter, unless you count that "four colors in one" pen as more than one. Is that right? like it, like it very very much. We go home to Tokyo happy, very happy. We take many pictures, ya.

Kyoshi Yashi Moshi
Japan

Me gustó mucho su obra. Yo crecí in Mexico, manijando un automóvil como ese que tiene dentro del garaje. Tengo solamente una queja. El otro dia (esta era nuestra segunda visita) por aquí andaba un negro, un hombre muy gordo, pesado, maloliente, que nos estorbaba ir dentro del bungalow. Parece que busquaba algo dentro del televisión. No dicimos nada porque no sabíamos, quizás era un trabajdor del museo. Pero hoy lo vimos otra vez, y no creyemos que trabaja aquí. Un hombre muy raro. Pero aparte de eso, nos encantó mucho su obra. Gracias.

Pablo & Anna Huijon
Guanajuato, MX

長野誠一：

ビルのどこかで漏れがあるらしいなあ。水の滴る音がしていたから。誰か調べておいた方が

いいだろう。それに寒すぎる、ここは。

borta S blr jablu'DI' reH   yIbah
Qa Qqu'nay'

October 31, 1998

Packrat heaven. I'm sure my good friend Josh would wallow in this place, all those
buckets and springs and hoses and scraps. The guy never throws anything away! I'll
definately tell him about this.

George Wan, Seattle

The little plastic green German shepherd in the laboratory (glass cabinet, second
shelf, in front of the Principles of Heliotropism) reminds me of my dog Asta, from
when I was a boy. Because of him I gained a reputation for being fearless. You see,
once when I was seven he led me away from home one day, chasing a rabbit into the
woods. My mother was frantic. I had been gone for hours. "We were tracking an
animal," I told her when I got back. She was surprised at how calm and collected I
was. Milliken's work evokes such a rush of nostalgia, so many countless memories
for me, Renée. I am transported. I wish you could read this today. I miss you.

John Wycliff, UK

Ahoj, kluci!

Est-qu'un club s'est formé autour de cette exposition? Je suis venu deux fois avec
ma maman ce weekend, et j'ai recontré la même femme un peu ronde qui regardait
furtivement dans les recoins du garage et qui écrivait dans un carnet. Est-ce que
quelqu'un dans cette ville travaille, ou est-ce qu'ils sout tous des mannequins et des
vendeuses? Ma mére a beaucoup apprecié le tome de De Beauvoir dans les toilettes.
Salutations.

Phillipe-Louis Anglade
Québec, CANADA

Meget god, men meget prætentiøs, især musikken og lydeffekterne. Jeg så jeres
udstilling "Pavillion" sidste gang, jeg rejste rundt på Vestkysten, og min reaktion
var nogenlunde den samme. Regnen virkede meget fjollet. Når en kunstner er
løbet tør for ideer, begynder han at bruge special effects. Denne udstilling hører
hjemme i Hollywood. De bedste hilsner,

Renate Dorff-Schultz, Holte, Danmark

Too many niggers.

180

November 3, 1998

Dear sirs,
My usual metier being restaurant critiques, I was dragged here against my will by an
LA acquaintance with whom I may never spend an afternoon again. Suffice it to say
that I would much rather have been elsewhere sampling the local cuisine. This
exhibit is trés vulgar, trés common and trés tasteless. It is a great big inflated soufflé
with nothing inside to recommend it. This is all sound and fury signifying nothing.
This "Americana," as it is usually termed, has finally lost whatever decadent charms
it might have possessed thirty years ago and descended into the merest camp, the
coarsest naturalism. I might also put in a word for larger doors. I could hardly
squeeze my dainty frame through the oppressive confines of the entrance. While
inside, what greeted me was hardly worth the effort. My former friend is finished at
last with her tiresome review of the proceedings, and my stomach is grumbling
intolerably. I wish you a most fond adieu, sir. May your escargots come al carbon,
may your profiteroles be flambéed. Only a culture raised on burgers and pizza could
create something like this and dare to call it "art." I remain ever

your most humble servant,
Roland Gastronome, Paris

N'ecoutez pas Roland. L'oeurve est magnifique. Bravo! Le gorille est parfait. Les
détails et la passion dans l'oeurve me donnent un désir ardent de manger des
carottes. Ne me demandez pas d'explication.

C. Troescher, Paris

We really enjoyed it, without being sure what we were supposed to get out of it.
The little blurb says you're Egyptian. Is Milliken an Egyptian name?

Lara Loyola, Austin, ID

It is extraordinary. We never thought Today I saw him. A man standing by the Dart,
huge, black, alone. He smelled. His breathing was heavy. A look of sadness in his
black black eyes as he stared vacantly at the exhibit. We locked eyes for just a split-
second. There was so much sadness there, so much loss and ignorance. It is he
whom we must help, Renée. To him must we bring peace, equality, as Milliken
brings peace and equality to these objects. I have been called an idealist but there is
nothing ideal in wanting the best for your country, for your fellow man, to give him
the ultimate gift, your love. We must help this man, and the countless masses just
like him. We must raise them. Only then will we truly be free. This invasion, the
political squabbles, they all fade in comparison to this supreme task: the integration
of the human race. extraordinary, extraordinary.

Heather Wells, Wanake, MN

Пусть всё это плохо, но своё, а ведь своё
говно не воняет.

Яра Горький
Москва

total loss. Best of luck in the future and think about what I said.

Roger Donner Clovis, NM

天安门广场烈士永垂不朽！　　　　解放西藏！

我不知道我看懂了没有。　　李军

Growing up in Montana, you don't get a chance to see stuff like this. I mean, we live in a place a lot like it Jan, Oh my God, you were here today. I think I saw that man too. ~~Kunta K~~ the guard said he's seen him here before. He was disgusting. Him and that other one in the note, the French guy? Couldn't get through the door? Uggh! I'm sorry, but these people should just stay home, lose weight, something. It spoils the museum experience to see them wobbling around. These drooling wheelchair people too. Why should we "help" them? They should do us a favor and let us keep our lunch ha ha! People should help themselves. Besides my Dad says they get plenty of tax money. I'm sorry to hear things are going badly in ~~Cheekas Czakos~~ in your country. I don't watch the news much. Gorilla in the radiator grill!! Nice to see you back. Love, R. malnutrition for kids from these school lunches and all. But thank you all the same.

Tara Lurch, Poughkeepsie, MO

Mi è piaciuto assai. Mi sono sentito come se fussi entrato in una macchina del tempo, anche se il perché, non ve lo so dire. Issa è la prima volta cà in America, però aggia conosciuto molti americani in guerra. La nipote mia studia a cà. E' stato molto bello. Vi ringrazio.

Gennaro Esposito, Napoli, Italia

68 baby doll limbs, 9 planets, 13 moons, 7 pieces of graffiti It was a travesty, this riot on the day of the 52nd anniversary of the October Revolution, when there should be parades, not disorder. I walked down Prikopy Street with my friends and kept silent while they shouted anti-government slogans. I was not afraid. I had confronted the Warsaw pact troops in August, asked them why they oppress their nationalities at home and why they come here, where there is no counter-revolution. But these slogans, they were stupid and vulgar, they help nothing. But when the topic came to Brezhnev I could not keep silent. They fell upon us, the police, when we tried to cross the cordon on Jindriška street. My head was grazed by a baton. Nothing serious. On this of all days, it was a crime. Nothing will stop the student strike now. In history there is a moment when something must happen. three nobs on the Sylvania, 14 stacks of newspaper, 3 baseball cards

Не знаю. Чего скажешь? Моя мама говорит, что американцы все пошляки, ну, иногда и я так думаю. Но в вашем творении не ~~~~ знаю. Мне трудно с словами. Мне всё ещё нравится.

ДА ПОШЛА ТЫ, ПИЗДА МОКРАЯ

БЛЯДЬ

Вера Платонова
Тамбов, Россия

Being/Nothingness

Det mindede mig og min kæreste om et sted vi sov engang hvor vi var på rygsækrejse gennem Zaire. Vi kom næsten ud for et røveri der, men min kæreste har det sorte bælte i karate. Så han smadrede fjæset på dem. Virker bilen stadig? Vi ville gerne se, om den kan køre. Held og lykke!

Camilla Looper, København, Danmark

88 paper clips, 136 buttons, 18 matches, 27 doll bodies, 17 doll heads Renée, please meet me somewhere. I need to see you. Talk. I believe I saw you on Tuesday. You wore a green dress, your red hair in band. You wrote in the book. I could not see immediately what you wrote, because you were with a group of people, perhaps tourists. I could not dare approach. Renée, if that was you, please, I must see you. Renée, I am confused. Surely you have seen by now that I am harmless answer please 33 rubber bands, 1,998 sheets of white paper, 547 sheets of post-it notes, 386

November 17, 1998

We couldn't, like, stop giggling. You had us all like, oh my god, like, awesome, like fire it up, girl, like Jan, I thought we had an agreement. No meetings, no face to face. Stop asking me to meet you. We have a good thing here — no messiness. Don't get weird on me. There's enough weirdos around already. I'm sure you can handle whatever's bothering you. Just never you mind, sugah. Still your friend, Renée PS. I didn't make it on a callback because they needed someone "older." I even offered to dye my hair (the part was for a Scottish girl, so I thought my red would cover it), but they said no. they wanted a natural black haired lassie. Go figure. PPS. Was it you who wrote about a parade or party or something? Was that in a code? The weather's been gogeous lately. I hope you had a nice Czeck parade if that was you. because, like, Trina's dad tried to molest her over Spring Break and like, oh, wow gotta go, cool!

Minnie Dryer   Venice Beach, CA

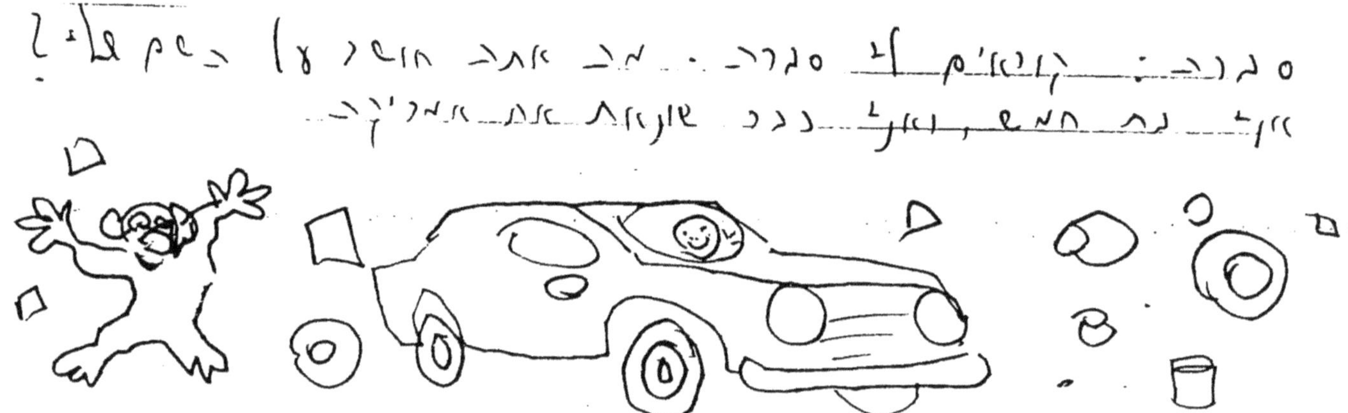

So'wI'vIchu'ta' HIjol qama'pu DIHoH net Sov

After flying 18 hours to make it here in time for my daughter's wedding, we just wanted to waste time until the dress was done R. I am sorry. This is the winter of discontent. The gorilla continues to elude me. J. glad we came here.

Aaron Herzl, Tel Aviv

Eye deed naught beleave inn fiendean duh fife remoat cuntrolls unteal Eye reekownted them fife thymes. De fad mann ease ah regoolrr Anne hee stings bat. Bud de garbs our awl FBI. Eat ist de psebundeenth dey too munchs Fromme my burrthmonth Anne Eye'm wading four Marie.

184

November 24, 1998

Andate tutti a fa'nculo, froci de merda. Ma chi pensate di fottere con tutte 'ste stronzate. Ve possino 'mazzà.

Vaccaro Romolo, Roma, Italia

This car reminds of the freeway today. It's not moving ha ha! And apart from Jan, just wanted to wish you a happy Thanksgiving. Im going to Scotland to be with my father and his wife. When do Czechs celebrate Thanksgiving? I hope it's this week too. I'll write sometime next week. I'm still amazed by all the new stuff I see in M.'s work, stuff that was right in front of me but I never noticed before, like the little Mexican wrestler thingie on the counter, and the Jayne Mansfield decal. Amazing what you can see when you just open your eyes, huh? Love, R. worth the trouble of gassing up twice. As you say, "a tribute to our automotive city."

Keyser Sozë Bugaria

Bravo! Vi syntes godt om det og fik os et godt grin. Det med babyen på loftet er sygt. Det var tæt på, at jeg efterlod noget. Hvem skal tørre alt det op? Haha.

Lars Smith-Poulsen, Nykøbing F., Danmark

関根美智子：

大好きでしたわ。日本にもツアーをしに来てください！是非見に行きますよ！

暗くて何もみえない。まるでお墓の中のよう。．．

C'est passionnant. Le mannequin dans le voiture m'a bien fait peur. Qu'est-ce c'est pour un type qui invente des choses pareilles? Et l'autre voiture-sculpture qui se trouve dans le couloir? C'est cradot tout ça-je me seus villaire de l'avoir vu. Merçi.

Aldo Kuenzli, Chartres

70 erasers, 14 hub caps, 3 typewriters (Welmington, Brother, GE), 2 microcopes, We must admit the obvious. The strike has failed. At last we were doing something, at last there was going to be a response to August. I had never felt more alive. But Strakhov is finished. They all bowed their heads. Svoboda, Dubcek, Smrkovsky, surely they cannot fail us now. Surely in them there still burns the spirit of the Spring. Surely there remain Czechs who want to do something, surely 6 Coca Cola bottles, 10 milk crates, one baby carriage, one gorilla (laughing under Dart), 63 glass

185

December 3, 1998

Las Vegas was better. They've got things like this, only they move and have lights. This gets rather boring. My wife agrees completely. Strange people visit here.

Herbert George Walls, Central City, UT

cras amet qui numquam amavit,
quique amavit cras amet

Las Vegas was better. They've got things like this, only Renee, I hope very much you came back today. The day approaches. Helen, Eva, Pavel do not really understand. Helen is more of a sister, a friend in need because of her illness. I feel I can speak with you, only you. At least tell me about you, your life, your references. I have your image burned in my mind, say you will respond agrees completely. Strange people visit here.

Herbert George Walls, Central City, UT

Much better than our own Kunsthauswien. This spectacle, this ready-made texturality, furthers the notion that, in O'Doherty words, "as modernism gets older, context becomes content." I also find myself thinking of Bakhtin and carnival, this dissolution of space and border. A theatre without a venue, discourse and spectacle, signifier and signified together, game and dream. And finally, ironically, to De Vere: all the world a stage, all of us merely players. Warmest regards,

Wolfgang Rommel, Vienna

ЧЕГО, СУКА?

Художник-то умеет на дерьме сметану собирать! Ничего!

Duchamp, Keinholz, now Milliken. What more can I say? Jan, please, no more asking personal details. Remember, no contacts, no flesh, no sound waves. This notebook, maybe the chat rooms once in a while, is all I can handle. Nobody really meets in LA anymore. Things are crazy and hectic enough. My career's priority number 1. People are like, fourth on the food chain, buddy. Let me give you some advice: try to think of relationships as "take-take." Always ask yourself: what can this person do for me? Is it worth my while to keep in touch? You and I have fun, Jan, let's keep it that way. OK? I have no room for people trying to impose their view of life on me.   I've thought this through, I got all the angles covered. Please don't try to be a sickie. Love, R. PS. Gorilla alert! Behind the lava lamp and wig dummy, southeast laboratory! What do I win? accolades, accolades.

Cathy Boothton Milwaukee, WI

December 4, 1998

Давно слышал о Вашей работе, и был очень рад наконец её увидеть. Не разочаровала. У нас мало таких талантов, таких пророков, как вы. Мне жалько только, что не можем познакомиться. Но если хотите, *если приедете,* позвоните мне в России. Даже могло бы быть Вам прибыльно. Мои телефон: 255-1782. Счастливо!

Антон Бунин
Санкт Петербу[рг]

Will you return to school? You should perhaps return to school. I was rereading our correspondence last night. Czechs do not celebrate "Thanksgiving." Czechoslovakia is not in Asia. It is located in Eastern Europe, sandwiched between Poland and East Germany on the North and Austria, Hungary amd the Ukraine in the south. We are a great civilization that has been conquered and reconquered by brutes, from the Western Catholic papists to the Nazi savages and now these Soviet scum, who proclaim themselves our brothers while they arrest us in hordes, beat us, stamp us down while the world turns its back on us yet again. And all we can do, the great Czech people, the heirs of Hus and Zizka and Masaryk, is bow our heads and swallow this slow, bitter poison. I am happy only that my father is not alive to see this day. Go to school, Renée. Learn what it means to be a human being. J.P.

岡田小百合：

別に分かっている訳ではないけれど奇麗だったわね。本当ですか、アメリカ人が人間の頭蓋骨を自分の車庫に取っておくのって。そう言えばいとこのことを思い出してしまって、彼女が可愛がっていた猫が死んでしまってもお別れするのができなくてね。だって、もう二十年間一緒に暮らしをしたんですもの。死体を廃棄したけれど、おいとまを告げるなんて耐えられなくて、ホルムアルデヒドで腐らせずに長持ちさせてから棚に置いておきましたわ。何年もそこにあったのよ。いとこの旦那さんが癌で亡くなってからというものしばしばそれとお話しするのね。ご主人は長崎市に近い街の出身だったけど幸いに原爆の日にはそこにいなかった。いとこはそこにいたけれど結局身体の方は無事だったのね。その彼女が亡くなってから猫の頭蓋骨もなくなったらしい。どうしたんでしょう。分からないわ。いとこの子供達が知っているのかもしれないけど。天皇陛下が飼っていらっしゃる一匹の猫の名にちなんで名づけられたそうだけれど、その名前、わたし、さっぱりと覚えていないんです。

My son and I did not appreciate the vulgar graffiti. Mr. Milliken, you, sir, are an arrogant elitist. Sincerely,

Roh-Min Wade NY, NY

December 13, 1998

We'se from Louisiana, but just never you mind, sugah. Cuz this here art is way beyond I don't get you, Jan. School? It's fine for you, you want to study law or whatever, but I've got the talent and the wilingness to make it in the entertainment biz. My agent Frank says I'm doing real well. That perfume commercial is coming out in Febuary in Italy, France, all over Europe. Probably in Cheskoslovia too. They're gonna see my face plastered all over the place. My career is moving right along. So don't be telling me what to do. What's school gonna do for me? I need info I can use right here, right now. I don't care if you're pissed off about your country or whatever. I don't care where it is. I live in America. If there's a war or something going on then maybe you just shouldn't go back. Just never you mind. Stay here. You might be happier. You're starting to act really weird. Your making me think that maybe this has gone on too long. R. PS. Why didn't you hide your message? Miss Jean Brodie smiled at me today, so I guess we got lucky. Still got her fooled. But you better be careful or this is over! for the gumbo in the pot. Thanke.

Greta Dupree
Shreveport, LA

让大家在这些本子上题字是很好的想法！不过这个年轻人让我
很长时间写不成。他一直在自己写。我非得等了又等直到他
离开。这合法吗？这个展览很不错。我下次进城一定会再
来看。如果这个年轻人还在这儿我会申诉。他得明白别人
也想写。此致敬礼，郭荣民

很好　　　　　← KИТАЙСКАЯ БЛЯДЬ 卐

Jeg syntes ikke så godt om dette som om den Marc Chagall-udstilling, der også findes i galleriet, eftersom denne udstilling - i modsætning til Marc Chagall-værkerne - er kitsch. Der er ikke lagt nogen følelse i værkerne, de er blot en meningsløs akkumulering af materiale. På et af skiltene stod "6 gulerødder, 2 vandmeloner, vaskepulver". Skulle det kunne berøre tilskueren følelsesmæssigt? Hr. McMillen burde indse, at det banale næppe kan være nogen inspirationskilde. Vi har haft den type værker i Europa og deres tid er forbi. Jeg var pinligt berørt over at måtte forklare min lille søn, hvad sætningerne på væggen betød. Museet burde sætte en advarsel op om den slags. Det er ikke Disneyland. Med venlig hilsen

Per Søndergaard, Ålborg, Danmark

December 22, 1998

Occupation. Beneš again. Capitulation. The reforms, the last year, erased, banished. No, we cannot repeat the Heydrich affair, that will only bring on another Lidice and Ležaky. These men are animals, I see that now. We are a proud, tiny people crushed between giants, and alone, always alone. No, we must not strike at them, but at our own national cowardice. But, God in Heaven, Kosmopolitas. Is this the only way? In Vietnam, perhaps, but here? Is this what we have come to? And yet. And yet. What is sealed in blood is sacred. For the martyrs of Lipany, for the Taborites, for Komenský, for Žižka, for our holy father Hus himself, we must not waver. These men had principles. They believed absolutely in their cause. They had no doubt. They proved that one man, or one group of unified men, can stand up to tyranny. They were the best, the flower of our nation. Their blood boiled but their spirit remained unbroken. I am proud to carry their name and their cause. I hereby place my name in the lots. My brothers, my father, you can rely on me. Truth prevails. As God is my witness, I will not fail you. Renée. The gorilla is hiding in the Sylvania again. He gibbers at me but I do not answer. I wish I could touch you, just once. J.P.

ВАШ ХУДОЖНИК СЕРУН. ВСЕ-ТАКИ ВЫСТАВКА НЕПЛОХА. ЗАЧЕМ ВСЕ ПИШУТ? ТАК ОХОТНО, ОХОТНО, ВСЕ В ОЧЕРЕДИ ТАКОЙ. Выразиться так важно, что ли? Это делать бессмысленно, хуй, то же, что пизде пить подавать. Ну, Всё. Чепуха такая, не надо пизду смешить.

Анатолий Кузмич
Рига

PATRONS ARE STRONGLY REQUESTED TO USE THIS SPACE ONLY FOR COMMENTS REGARDING THE MILLIKEN EXHIBIT. THIS IS LACMA PROPERTY AND UNAUTHORIZED USE IS PROHIBITED.

THANK YOU.

— Tara Wort, hall security

Show is good in the hall. My family likes the show. It is berry orijinal. we think to the lady who cums in here and rites in the book. Miss, my name is Hollis, the security guard. Black guy. We have to talk about your freind. Pleez see me as soon as posible. Ax for me at the counder. Say it is urgent and I will knoe it is you. H.M. like it berry berry much. Weere from Meksico. Like it berry much.

Raul Ganja, Meksico

December 23, 1998

Zajímavé, velmi zajímavé.   Ale jedný veci nerozumím. Proč jste povesil ty panenky ze stropu? A co mají společnyho s garaží? Vypadalo to divně, zvláštně. To auto tady mi připomenulo to, které měl můj strýc za války. Byla to Tatra. Měl ji dlouho a šlapala dobře.

Zdeněk Novotný, Praha

Господи, меня так напугал один чёрный такой, в „лаборатории". Слышала там музыку а вот подполз. Страшен он такой. Я уж пожилая, мне не надо такие ужасы. Штуку платила за поездку. Шесть дней, шесть ночей с питанием два раза в день. А мой сын, вот, не любит что я

Jan. That's it. It's over. The security guard told me that you've been acting really weird, that you've been standing inside the exhibit everyday, all day, for a week now. That your mumbling all the time or something. I'm not going in there. When you see this, don't write me again. I'm not coming back. Get help, man. That's all I can say. R.

我从来没见过这种东西。美国人真是肤浅无知。

你以为这种玩意儿就能让你逃过生死大劫？应该

学着生活在自然和谐里，敬老扶少，别想着这些破烂。

玩意儿是指小孩子的。我看这儿就是一个玩具屋子。这个艺术

家不是50岁，而是5岁。谁要认为这是艺术谁就头脑有

问题。

YOUR ASS SUCKS CANAL WATER

Boner11 says, "I am long and strong ready and for fricSHONN."
Gonerill says, "over the weekend TIA"
SarahHeartburn says, "HA HA Lance never you mind"
LEONLEVY ENTERS.
APHRODESIAFOXX ENTERS.
MODERNMACHO LEAVES, HEADED FOR LORD DUNCENEY'S PLACE.
16J69 ENTERS.
Famine says, "Oral why don't you like Guinan? Because her name sounds too much like vagina?"
Augiewren says, "fuck speilburg"
SarahHeartburn says, "your birthday suit and I'll be in mine ;-)"
QUASIMODO77 ENTERS.
NANCYFANCY AND STEVE88 EXECUTE A TRIPLE AXEL.
Keiko says, "anybody feeling smurfy tonite?"
Coldfire says, ":-ss :-E @>--,--- :*)"
Korkie says, "aadriaaaaaaaaaaann"
Gesamkunstwerk says, "dieser Theorie kann man aber entgegenhalten"
Hurl13 says, "i got my name fom the song."
PETERHUTCH ENTERS.
H2O4U LEAVES, HEADED FOR SCIENCE FAIR #3.
16J69 says, "Renee, this is Jan."
CABA says, "Just go home to my den of thieves"
BONER11 OFFICIALLY DECLARES HIMSELF AN UP-ALL-NIGHT CHAT DEMIGOD.
DanPussey80 says, "No fat chicks."
Coldfire says, "boredom and socialism."
76* says, "save the speeches for Malcomlm-X. i just wanna get laid laid laid laid"
SarahHeartburn says, "Jan? Oh, hi Jan. No Digstorm, it cost $70."
ASPCLASP ENTERS.
SLOWSTROKE LEAVES, HEADED FOR UP-ALL-NIGHT CHAT ALLEY #2.
RAZZLE ENTERS.
Coldfire says, "8-)"
Hurl13 says, "Walk this Way."
ChrisDivine says, "It was the name of a Czech princess, Quecho."
YOUNGBERRY ENTERS.
SCABFREE ENTERS.

UP-ALL-NIGHT CHAT/ JANUARY 15, 1999

STEELROD LEAVES, HEADED FOR INTERNATIONAL ALLEY.
Granta says, "didn't care fr it. B-)"
16J69 says, "Renee are you receiving my messages?"
Crusty889 says, "do you like wrestling (sport)"
Famine says, "anyone out here from Iowa?"
4049U says, "cabron ya te di una vez."
STEELROD LEAVES.
MORPHEUS40 LEAVES.
SarahHeartburn says, "Jan can't write too busy lotsa PMs"
Ubermensch says, "have to 'fess up Carl"
Candycando says, "uh uh uh"
Kiko says, "LOL LOLLOLOLOL"
PREGNUN LEAVES.
DOCILESOUL ENTERS.
LONGDONG ENTERS.
BONER11 LEAVES, HEADED FOR DAYCARE CENTRAL.
Bacchanalia says, "no, ron, %-)"
16J69 says, "Renee, please let us go to a private room"
FinFangFoom88 says, "No comeback, Lilley?"
Praxis says, "wiggle and wobble when they cum"
Quecho says, "saw disney"
Sisko31 says, "bortaS blr jablu'DI'reh QaQqu'nay'"
BOULDERBALLS ENTERS.
798J ENTERS.
HUNGWELL ENTERS.
Coldfire says, "50 fucking pages??"
Jos23 says, "Never finish"
Quecho says, "Mbello que edad tenes?"
16J69 says, "Renee, please let us talk in private room or give me
your number"
LanceCarbuncles says, "all women in this room bend over NOW"
THULE ENTERS.
LISHA16 LEAVES, HEADED FOR ICE CREAM PARLOR.
EPIPHANY26169 LEAVES.
Nettuno says, "te acuerdas de mi"
Mechoui says, "yeah fat chicks suck — literally LOL"

UP-ALL-NIGHT CHAT/ JANUARY 15, 1999

FULVING LEAVES, MOONING THE ROOM, HEADED FOR CHAT ALLEY.

Mentosing says, "18 hours is long time to type"

Famine says, "Prozack, where did you go."

SarahHeartburn says, "Pass the Red Stripe yall. Jan busy later"

Llopis says, "Hi Rockin, pull my finger"

POET100 LEAVES, HEADED FOR INTERNATIONAL.

ALEXANDRA X AND GECKO GET IT ON BY THE BAR.

Triack says, "Matlock, Baretta and the Hendersons"

TB68 says, "si, si, cosi, cosi, cosi"

Resilient says, "good one SarahH LOL"

Ostrichprick says, "sugarbabay you a man or a woman"

SHAON691 ENTERS.

Mbello says, "til it dried up"

SarahHeartburn says, "Jan enough awready Praxis, that's gross"

Funnyegyptncamel says, "8:-) :-*"

ASPCLASP LEAVES, GIVING COLDFIRE THE FINGER.

DARIUS ENTERS.

SHOSHONE ENTERS.

Chestmolester says,"8th grade."

SarahHeartburn says, "Jan, stop PMing me"

Valleygay says, "Pepino your going to feel like shit tomorrow"

FRANCINE7 ENTERS.

DODO LEAVES.

LEONLEVY LEAVES, HEADED FOR CHURCH.

Jos23 says, "Sam won't mind"

Mirrostage says, "is it ralph or rafe?"

Turdburger says, ":-@ :-@ :-@ :-@ :-@ :-@ :-@ :-@ :-@ :-@ :-@ :-@ :-@ :-@ :-@"

THULE LEAVES.

CHIPG LEAVES.

LanceCarbuncles says, "you ain't got it in the hips you better have it in the lips."

SarahHeartburn says, "Jan pissing me off serious"

Julie41 says, "oh, do you think she really meant it? sometimes they just says that"

Funnyegyptncamel says, "K:P C=}>;*{)) CU"

UP-ALL-NIGHT CHAT/ JANUARY 15, 1999

PepeP says, "odin Tviks, pozhayulsta"
COLDFIRE LEAVES.
SARAHHEARTBURN LEAVES, HEADED FOR PRIVATE ROOM
Boulderballs says, "you can take the but you ca't"
Cathystrap says, "going to bed"

16J69 YOU HAVE LEFT CHATHOUSE ROMANCE #57, HEADED FOR PRIVATE ROOM
16J69 YOU HAVE ENTERED PRIVATE ROOM

16J69: Are you there?

SarahHeartburn: Okay, here we are.

16J69: Is your attention fully in here?

SarahHeartburn: Yes yes

16J69: Sorry to drag you away from there

SarahHeartburn: Jan, what do you want

16J69: You are angry

SarahHeartburn: I thought we were going to keep this fun

16J69: Renee, I'm scared

SarahHeartburn: What are you taking about

16J69: What is sealed with blood is sacred.

SarahHeartburn: Say what?

16J69: What is sealed with blood is sacred. Everyone denouncing,
turning in their friends. The winter so cold, dark. They see
tanks and even Dubcek caves in why why I am not What is sealed
with blood is sacred.

SarahHeartburn: Jan, i don't know what you're talking about and I
dont care. I told you in that book that it's over

16J69: What is sealed with blood is sacred. There must be
sacrifices. mother, there must be sacrifices you must understand

SarahHeartburn: Jan, this isn't funny at all. This is not the way
to make up with me I'm warning you

UP-ALL-NIGHT CHAT/ JANUARY 15, 1999

16J69: Maminko, if you had read Capek's Mother you would know,
that there always must be sacrifices what is sealed with blood is
sacred

SarahHeartburn: I'm going to get off now. your sick

16J69: They'll see. They'll understand.   What is sealed with
blood is sacred. This will shine the path for them all. We must
not only have great thoughts, we must not only be able to
pronounce them. We must be able to realize them. It is horrible
but it must be done What is sealed with blood is scared.

SarahHeartburn: Don't write me anymore

16J69: For Opletal, for Hus, for Zµzka. It must be done. What is
sealed with blood is sacred. What is sealed with blood is sacred
Ren help me.

SarahHeartburn: Leave me alone. I hate you. Don't ever write me
again, you sick fuck. This town is full of liars, sickos Fuck
off, asshole

SARAHHEARTBURN LEAVES, HEADED FOR CHAT ALLEY
SARAHHEARTBURN IS NO LONGER LOGGED ON TO UP-ALL-NIGHT CHAT

16J69: ds984

16J69: fd98tIEU893T O289dfihd57

16J69 DO YOU WISH TO CONTINUE?

16J69 YOU HAVE BEEN IDLE FOR SOME TIME.   DO YOU WISH TO CONTINUE?

16J69:

16J69: The number of conflicts is not only growing, but some
conflicts are becoming perpetual (e.g., Vietnam). Humanity is
going astray, its existence is in its own hands and a change in
its consciousness (the mentality of humanity) is one of the vital
conditions for the furtherance of human life. Otherwise the
monstrous powers which man has constructed will destroy their
creator. It — this transformation of consciousness — is therefore
necessary, for only a self-aware humanity (self-aware in toto) is
capable of resolving the fundamental divisions (political,
ideological, social, and cultural) of today's society. Once it

UP-ALL-NIGHT CHAT/ JANUARY 15, 1999

has surmounted these divisions, humanity will achieve balance with
itself, and start on a path of much faster advancement than today.

16J69: In this stage humanity would stride forth as an integrated,
homogenous entity, distinguished by the expeditious development of
its thinking, the realization of gigantic projects

16J69: Obstructing this unity, however, are political, economic,
ideological, and other impediments. But humanity, if it wants to
live, must realize this integration

16J69: 9jggr3\84tt9=

16J69: d9fids-=4t6+n0IREKoity969

16J69:

16J69:

16J69:

16J69: Because our nations are on the brink of despair we have
decided to express our protest and wake up the people of this
land. Our group is composed of volunteers who are willing to
burn themselves for our cause. It was my honor to draw lot number
one and thus I acquired the privilege of writing the first letter
and starting as the first torch. Our demands are:

     1) immediate elimination of censorship,
     2) prohibition on the distribution of Zpravy.

If our demands are not fulfilled within five days by January 21,
1969, and if the people do not support us sufficiently through a
strike of indefinite duration, more torches will burn. Remember
August. In international politics a place was made for
Czechoslovakia. Let us use it.

               — Torch Number One

16J69 YOU HAVE LEFT PRIVATE ROOM, HEADED FOR CHAT ALLEY
16J69 YOU ARE NO LONGER LOGGED ON TO UP-ALL-NIGHT CHAT
    SEE YOU SOON!

UP-ALL-NIGHT CHAT/ JANUARY 15, 1999

'Performance Art' Turns Deadly

by Jackie Swann
LA Times Staff

(Jan. 17) Another bizarre suicide, this time outside the Los Angeles County Museum of Art, shocked residents and tourists Saturday, reigniting concern that a new wave of millenium-inspired mass suicides might be in store for the city.

A Hispanic male, 20-25 years old, set himself ablaze before stunned gallery visitors in the LACMA's central Rupert Murdoch courtyard at about 3 p.m., during the museum's busiest afternoon period and in the middle of a performance by the West African Yoruba House Band.

"He poured gasoline on himself, then just lit a match and WHOOP! up he went," said Gerry Bonior, a tourist from Evanston, IL. "It sounded like a big blanket being flapped, you know, a big whoosh. He looked really calm."

Security staff immediately evacuated visitors and extinguished the flames, but the man suffered burns over 85% of his body and was declared dead on arrival at LA County Hospital. Witnesses said the man was conscious after the flames were put out, and trying to speak.

"He was mumbling something about reports, or something, coming in from all over the country," said Belle Abbal, a museum staff member. "I heard him say very clearly, 'I am not a suicide!' It was horrible."

LAPD detective Karl Freund said the police believes this to be the act of a disturbed individual and not part of a new series of suicides. Officials are anxious to allay fears in light of last summer's epidemic of self-inflicted deaths and mass suicides, most of them blamed on apocalyptic hysteria surrounding the new millennium.

"The last thing we want the public to think is this is Rancho Santa Fe or the Universal Studios thing all over again," said Freund. "This man was clearly acting alone. He was apparently under the delusion that this was 'performance art.'"

But there is strong evidence that the man might have planned the incident with others for at least the last few months, according to several museum staff members who said they had seen him come in often and who believed he might have been communicating with someone else through one of the gallery's visitor notebooks.

"He was a regular," said Tara Wort, who oversees security in the museum's Armand Hammer building. "We get folks like him. He would come in day in, day out, write in the book, stare at the artwork. There's more like him than you think."

The man spent most of his time studying one work, the "installation" piece "Central Meridian" by Santa Monica artist Michael Milleken, on the second floor of the museum's Burt Ward hall. Milleken could not be reached for comment.

One museum worker, who refused to be named, said the man was corresponding with a woman and possibly one other person through the notebook, which lies on a podium accessible to the public, inside the hall. The worker refused to elaborate.

The LAPD confiscated the visitor's notebook and is currently examining it for clues, Freund said. The deceased man's identity is being withheld pending notification of next of kin, though officials did confirm the man was an actor and a Los Angeleno.

Adding to the surreal nature of the event, most bystanders at first thought the incident was an "art action" or "publicity stunt" for the upcoming *Fantastic Four* movie, which premieres Feb. 28 — until it became obvious that the man was really on fire.

"I thought it was, like, part of the ticket price," said Cameron Croix, of Phoenix, AZ. "We were like, 'Hey, look at that. Cool. 'Flame on,' dude.'"

"There was no warning, no announcement, so I knew this was either part of the African cultural program or something else, something seriously wrong," added Ethel Krolik, of Hampstead, England. "Our trip has certainly been made memorable now, hasn't it?"

The Yoruba House Band continued its performance shortly after the victim's evacuation. The musicians recited a short prayer for the man's welfare.

LACMA's 'Human Torch' Believed Himself Reincarnated Protester

by Huey Planchet
L.A. Examiner

(Jan. 18) The man who burned himself to death at the Los Angeles County Museum of Art on Saturday acted under the belief that he was a 1960s protester from Eastern Europe, police said yesterday.

Juan Dunlap, 27, a local theater actor, set himself on fire in an open-air breezeway before unsuspecting tourists in an attempt to recreate the self-immolation (suicide by fire) of Jan Palach, a 20-year-old student who protested the 1968 Soviet invasion of Czechoslovakia by setting himself ablaze in 1969, police revealed.

"He sent a letter to the city government the day of the incident explaining why he did it, which was exactly, word for word, like Palach's suicide note," said police chief Gil Hrandt. "That, plus his last words, helped us solve the mystery."

Police also received calls from throughout the country after the incident was reported in the national news, which helped establish the bizarre event's significance.

"I was completely bamboozled when I saw it, when I realized the date and the time and everything else," said Frantisek Grozs, a professor of Slavic Languages at UCLA. "He matched everything perfectly, down to the clothes, the time of day. I've never heard of anything like this."

Jan. 16 was the 30th anniversary of the Palach suicide, which took place on Prague's Wenceslas Square in the wake of the Soviet Bloc's reversal of Czechoslovak liberal reforms known as the "Prague Spring." Palach is considered a martyr and hero to the Czech people. There is no other known instance of someone copying his act so precisely. Dunlap allegedly even managed to run the same number of steps while on fire as Palach did.

Dunlap, originally from Rolling Rock, Texas, was a bit actor in the local theater scene, although he had not worked professionally for at least two years. He had a history of depression and antisocial tendencies, said Ward Woodrow of the fringe theater Polanski's Puppets. Dunlap had previously starred in a one-man show based on Palach in Texas, "but I heard it was pretty bad," he added.

Most specialists agree that Dunlap suffered from "extreme identification" or *"Single White Female* Syndrome," perhaps brought on by extreme depression, mental illness, or stress.

"Because our nations are on the brink of despair we have decided to express our protest and to wake up the people of this land ... In international politics a place was made for Czechoslovakia. Let us use it," read part of Dunlap/Palach's note, in which he referred to himself as "Torch Number One."

The Czech consulate had no comment on the tragedy.

Dunlap had in recent weeks approached the museum about staging an "action" in the building's breezeway, but was refused several times, said LACMA executive director Harry Bergson. Dunlap, a frequent visitor to the gallery and well-known to the staff, would sometimes spend hours a day inside one of the museums "installation" pieces.

"We need to check people's driver's licenses, passports, something," said security chief Tara Wort. "This sort of thing is just going to happen again and again."

Indeed, there is some concern that Dunlap's act might initiate a "historical suicide" fad in the city, although some hair-splitters pointed out that Dunlap failed to duplicate the 1969 incident in all its details. Dunlap died en route to the hospital, while Palach expired a full three days after setting himself on fire.

"I guess you can't really control that," said Fred Dern, president of the LA chapter of the Society for Creative Anachronism. "But it was still quite a re-creation. I heard that inside the ambulance he was saying Palach's last words down to the letter, verbatim. Whoa. You can't get more post-modern than that."

Dunlap's apartment was found to be full of Palach and Czech memorabilia, Hrandt added. Dunlap's family refused to comment on the death. His body will be cremated in a private ceremony in Eagle Pass, Texas on Wednesday, according to a spokesman.

Despite reports that Dunlap was acting in conjunction with a "woman" he wrote letters to through one of LACMA's visitor's comments notebooks, the police said Saturday they consider the case closed.

They returned the notebook to the museum yesterday, saying they found no concrete evidence of a conspiracy.

(Variety — LA, Jan. 21) Gold Calf Entertainment has inked a $2 mil deal to produce a television mini-series on the life of Juan Dunlap, the small-time actor who burned himself to death outside the Los Angeles County Museum of Art last Saturday. The story, based on details supplied by Tara Wort, security chief at LACMA, promises "spicy sex and digitally enhanced computer generated effects" during the climactic burn scene, according to Gold Calf. Production is slated to begin in early March, under director Ciaran Gere, who is attached with Manna Productions. Location shooting will take place in LA, with set work at the Warner Bros. studios. Second unit production is scheduled for New Orleans.

"That Big Easy feel will capture perfectly the look of exotic Hungary, where that other one, the real guy died," said Gere, who last year produced the popular Goat Brains video, *Suck Your Love Out of Me.* "It's gonna rock. Sap has already guaranteed me a song for it." Gere is currently in negotiations with Trent Reznor to produce the series soundtrack.

Dunlap died believing he was a European protester from 1979. Joaquin Phoenix, originally slated to star as the troubled actor, ankled from the project yesterday after a contract dispute. Gere and Manna are currently looking for an unknown to play the demanding role. Look for *Light My Fire: The Juan Dunlap Story* to run on NBC during the May sweeps. — *Regina Starr*

Comet Boy Returning to Earth!

In an incredible new chapter to the story of Juan "Human Torch" Dunlap, psychics this week revealed that the spirit of the tragic LA suicide, who set himself on fire because of his homosexuality, is shooting back to Earth from space at 100,000 miles per hour! The stunning news was confirmed by astronomers, who reported seeing the Hale-Bopp comet stop, twist, and suddenly change course to once again intersect the Earth! It should arrive late this year, when Dunlap will leap from the comet and streak across the sky, they said.

"He feels his mission on this plane is not yet finished," said psychic Nora Veil of the International Paranormal Center in Tuskegee, IL. "He originally wanted to join the Heaven's Gate astronauts on the comet, but the widespread sympathy for him back home has made him change his mind."

In another amazing discovery, the *Weekly National Star* has learned that astronomers actually snapped photos of Dunlap on board the comet spacecraft! The pictures show the burned teenager waving to his former planet with HG leaders Marshall Applewhite and Bonnie Nettles as well as Elvis standing by his

January 20, 1999

We were very sorry to hear about this young man, Dunlap. It really is a wonderful work, but to kill oneself over it is something I don't think we'll ever understand. He was young, he had so much ahead of him. What is the world coming to?

Barbara Rattle Muncie, IN

SHOVE A STEER
IN YOUR REAR
WITH A SPEAR DEEPER DEAR **WITH A JEER** AND A LEER

DRINK YOUR BEER
WITH A TEAR

FUCKIN FAGiTS

If you are still coming to read, pleez see me. I have something for you from J. Ax for me at the fron counder. Say it is urgent. You knoe who you are. H.M.

HEAR HEAR!
IS THIS WHAT THEY CALL A WRITING CAREER?
YES, IF YOU'RE QUEER
OR NORMAN LEAR
OR THE MAN WITHOUT FEAR
WIPE YOUR SMEAR

You should not allow these booklets in the hall. We have small children with us and just look at the filth on this page. Now you have people burning themselves up in the galleries. Why do you encourage these activities? Our pastor spoke out against this museum and now we see why. It's all part of the apocalypse, like they said on the news. Well, my family has the Lord and we're safe. We will look down from Heaven at the rest of you and laugh while you all burn in hell forever like that crazy man last week.

Gary Fang, Inglewood

Hark, Methinks mine Romeo is near
>Last night I was licking an 8-year-old girl's pussy for one hour.

You are a sonofabitch

Mr. Milliken: You know, of course, that it was your fault that boy killed himslf. You should dismantle that monstrosity and give up this harmful profession. You artists don't realize the effect your work has on fragile minds and sensitive natures. You are just another Hollywood hack trying to get recognition as a serious "artist" but you forget that this is not a game. People do respond and you have a responsibility

200

January 23, 1999

Dear Juan,

Today Hollis gave me the envelope you left for me, the one that had the chat session print-outs and our pages from the LACMA book. Hollis said you came in the morning of your suicide to give him the envelope. Hollis asked if you were okay and said that I had been worried about you (a lie), but you had no reaction, he said. You gave him the envelope and didn't go in to the exhibit. Since you weren't doing anything unusual and you didn't want to talk to him, Hollis couldn't stop you and you walked out. He's a nice guy, Hollis. He was really concerned about you and felt, I think, worse than anybody about what happened — even though he knew the least. Yes, he had been reading our messages, but only sporadically and not completely understanding.. I don't have that excuse. You died a week ago, and today I think I understand why. And that makes me feel ashamed, and stupid and a cold, useless, ugly bitch.

Juan, I want to be honest with you. My real name is Carla. I'm black. I'm 37, five feet, one inch tall, and weigh 162 pounds. I work as a temp, have been since I moved out to LA ten years ago. My parents, originally from Boston, put me through two years of Dartmouth before cutting me off, because they said I was lazy and stupid. I studied art. I didn't go home for my father's funeral. He died of a stroke. In the shower. He was not cremated. I used to get pleasure from the idea of his stinking, rotting corpse stuffing the worms. But not anymore. They make the coffins too good for that, anyway. No worms.

I want to be honest with you, Juan. That's all I want now. I need to be. So I have to tell you everything. Everyday I get up.

I go to work. Toyota Corolla, 1981, still works pretty good.
After work I come home.   I live alone. I had a bird but it
died. I come home, eat take-out (there's a cheap Chinese place
down the street, or else Wendy's or KFC or Burger King or Big
Kahuna or Mickie Dee's or Pizza Hut or Curio's or Jack in the Box
or Shoshoney's or Texadelphia or TGIF Friday's or Taco Quemado or
Lalo's or Sudden Pasta or Fatburger or Tony's or Cicio's or Jane's
American or Sal's Famous or Capone's or Denny's or Sambo's or
Crusty's or Mama's or Amy's or Spot Burger or Pato's or Yang Chow
or Ali Baba or Bugsy's or Juan's or Subway or Ay Caramba or
Strizzi's or Shamrock's or Taco Hell or Dynamite or Gina's or Toy
or Ramiro & Sons or Durango or Mosh Pit or La Salsa or Long John's
or Jade Palace or Hamburger Hamlet or Miller's Barbecue or Hamas
or Szechuan City or Double Clutch or Le Casbah or Fenton's or
Mel's or Happy Burrito or Red Tomato or Torta Loca or Arthur's or
Taco Cabana or O'Brien's or G.M. Steakhouse or Cholesterol or
China Explosion or Great Wall or Burns' or Spike's or No. 14 or
Klieglights or Charlie Chaplin's or Clint's or Basta Pasta or
Spuds and Suds or Enchilada Heaven or Tannebaum's or Grease Monkey
or Blake's or Chik Fil'a or Gatti's or Terminal Cancer or

     I sit and watch TV and eat some more. Working as a temp gives
me lots of time off. I only work if I feel like it. I try to
save up enough money so I don't have to work for months. Just stay
home. Order out. My kitchen floor is covered with old newspaper.
Sometimes I pee on myself. All the windows are sealed with caulk,
curtained. I hear the neighbors, their dog dragging himself along
my ceiling like a worm. I watch TV, a little 20 incher, color,
Sylvania, that gets great reception. I don't care about cable or
HDTV. There's always something on. I smoke and eat and fart and

belch and bite my nails and watch. There's always a flicker in
the room, a blue flicker of TV waves. It looks like a disco-
theque from the dark alley outside. I'm a virgin. I want to be
honest with you, Juan. I almost wrote Jan.

    In the evenings if I feel like it I surf. Sometimes I lurk, but
mainly I'm a flirting, laughing Rita-Hayworth-as-Gilda prick-
teasing goddess. I rush and whirl through the chat rooms. One
night last week I got 713 personal messages in one session. I was
having eight different conversations in five rooms, at once.
That's not all. I fuck at 33 baud. Netsex, cybercunt, webwhore.
All of me. I'm Renée, the red-haired, sassy supermodel. The
actress, the cooze who sells perfume in Europe and stops traffic
in Hong Kong. The lunches, the agents, the contacts. I must kill
and eat your children. Fuck me 'til I scream, sugah. Renée, nice
to meet you. I'm thin, 6'1", 115, tits and ass. My pussy smells
like lavender. I bathe in coconut milk. My skin is soft, very
pale, with just the lightest touch of freckles, like little pink
shadows from an overhead branch. My long red hair is curly,
tousled, wild, all my men like it that way. I like it that way.
Just like I've always had it, like when I ran across the hills of
Scotland to my Daddy on the porch to show him a sand dollar and
suck a lollipop on his knee while the swing swung. Yeah, my hair,
that's the real moneymaker. The real ball-drainer. It reaches
down my back, thick, it smells up the room with roses, splashes
red onto my white titties. My nipples are light pink splotches
the shape of seashells, all buttery, silky, Botticelli. Firm,
perky, 22 forever. Do you like me? Do you love me? Are you
hard? Should I tell you the rest of me? My ass, white and tight
as a soft, suede leather drum. I'm Renée. Hips wide, Andie

McDowell hips. I'm purring. I'm Renée. Just for you. I'm
breathing, hard. All of me. My chest is heaving. I'm on fire.
For you, baby, just for you. Legs, firm, soft, creamy, a
birthmark on the inside of my thigh, my left thigh, just for you.
My soft red pussy hairs shaven in a triangle, waiting for your
touch. A tattoo, a vermilion butterfly with heart-shaped wings, on
my right shoulder blade, it flies out sometimes from its red
forest, makes me giggle like a little girl. I'm Renée. Oh. Oh.
I'm what they want, what they all want. I'm what you want. *I'm
what every white boy off the Lake wants.* I'm everything. I'm
American pie. I'm red-haired and freckled and naked and open and
dripping and waiting, waiting, waiting for you, only for you. Oh,
I'm perfect and frozen and exactly what you need. Men look at me
and melt. I'm Renée. Fuck me, America. Oh, fuck me with all
your dicks in all your 50 states, squirt it all into me, every
last drop. Get it all out of your system. I can take it. I can
take it all I can I can I can

No. I want to be honest with you, Juan. I'm Carla. I have
fingers shaped like yams, like wrinkled black cucumbers. I'm not
Renée. My cunt is foul and empty, a black tangle. I want to be
honest with you, Juan. My armchair stinks from years of sitting
on it, farting, pissing on it. The whole apartment, it reeks of
me. When I don't work I do nothing. Nothing. I let myself rot.
Month after month, nothing changes except the smell. It gets
worse.

Oh God Juan I hate myself I hate I hate I hate I hate I hate I
hate I hate I hate I hate I hate I hate I hate I hate I hate I
hate I hate I hate I hate I hate I hate I hate I hate I hate I
hate I hate I hate I hate I hate I hate I hate I hate

Today I went to the library. Juan, I went back to school.

I read up some on Palach's last days. I wanted to find out all I could about him, about you. You probably know he was lucid for a good deal of the time, those three days in the hospital. It's the physical details I keep thinking of, those endless tiny details, like a painting. A black painting of charred, screaming flesh. Doctors consider burn cases hopeless when half the victim's body has been exposed to fire. You, exactly like Palach, had burns on over 85% of your body. Bravo. The details. So perversely, deliciously, mesmerizingly grisly. The whole body swells up in the first few hours, like a frankenfurter over a flame — or like my thumb, I guess, when a firecracker blew up in my hands when I was a little girl. First my thumb was the color of vanilla ice cream, all sweaty and shiny, then it turned gray, then purple. With third-degree burn victims the blistered skin, all dehydrated and seared, soon sloughs off to reveal live, tender, damaged tissue, sizzling beneath. The victim goes into "burn shock": normal blood flow is diverted from the brain, heart, and other vital organs to the skin, in a desperate effort to replenish the fluid-starved layers. There can be lots of inner damage too. When clothes drenched in gasoline are set aflame, the vapors they produce get inhaled and destroy the larynx and pharynx. The vocal cords and respiratory organs are completely burned, decimated, razed. Fire in your throat, your lungs, lighting up, violating the deepest recesses of your body. I can hardly imagine it. The pain of course, is unimaginable. Meanwhile, the destruction of the outer organism plays on in its own hellish symphony. The metabolic system, thrown into total confusion, can't cope with the new state of the body and breaks down like an overheated engine.

The victim starts to produce poisonous substances, foul yellow-
black liquids and white pus, as the body reaches a state called
"alternation," accompanied by more severe shock. It's almost like
it stops trying to heal itself, and instead seeks to hasten its
own destruction, to end the horrible agony. One big exposed wound,
it frantically retreats from life. As for what happens mentally,
we can only speculate. The metabolic changes and rerouted blood
flow seem to induce a form of madness, an altered consciousness, a
hallucinogenic state. Personality itself is burned away. The
patient, if he's outwardly aware, grows extremely sensitive to
stimuli, like noise, light, air. They become unbearable to him.
Once again a newborn, he is assaulted by a million incom-
prehensible sensations.

  .I didn't hear your dying words, Juan, but I know what they are,
or what they should have been. Doctors treating Palach first
heard him say, "I am not a suicide!" and later on he asked for
tea. The boy amazed everybody with his bravery, his honesty.
Here was a 20-year-old kid, burned beyond recognition, and he
never once complained about the pain. He was not drugged so
heavily that he lost consciousness, awareness, but by the same
token the pain was greater. His mood wavered back and forth those
72 hours from a "feeling of fulfillment" to anxious wondering
about the public's response to his act and finally, to depression
when he found out the people did not follow his lead and the
government did not cave in to his demands. The Saturday morning
after the deed he had the nurse hold the newspapers up to his
eyes, which were reduced to tiny chinks peeping out of swollen
skin, to see the evidence for himself. There, in that hospital
ward filling up with flowers, in a country jarred into shock and

grief — but not action — Jan Palach's faith was shaken. "I believe that our nation is no longer in need of light," he said. That evening his condition deteriorated rapidly. The doctors tried various token treatments, and he held on through the next morning. The more reliable of the two accounts of his final words describes his expressing the wish that others should not emulate his deed. By then he could hardly speak; he whispered each word slowly, every syllable a sharp, stabbing pain: "My act has fulfilled its purpose ... but no one else should do it or repeat it ... today our problems are great and seem insurmountable ... let this serve as the reason to maintain the struggle." His last words — and yours — were that we would all, somewhere, see each other again. Jan Palach died at half-past three on Sunday, January 19, 1969.

That's why I write this. That's why I'm typing out this letter to a dead, mad actor. I want to be honest with you, Juan. You gave me your truth, through your lies, and I want to give you mine. I needed to learn more about you, I had to, and I didn't want to wait for the goddamn television movie. I called your family in Texas, I wanted to ask them about you, about everything, but they hung up. They must be sick of phone calls, sick of everything. You were cremated, Juan, your ashes scattered I don't know where. Will we, somewhere, see each other again, I wonder. That, too, is why I write this. That gives me the strength, Juan. The strength to give you the truth. You do want the truth, don't you? Juan, I'm not Carla. Juan, my real name is Carl.

You saw me. You son of a bitch. Did you know it? Did you feel it? You must have, when you said, "We must help this man, and the countless masses just like him. We must raise them. Only then will we truly be free." You did mean that, didn't you, Juan? Even as you gagged on my reek and held back your sick at my bloated body, you never turned away, and you meant every word. Man, you meant all that shit, always. I understand that now. You wanted to resurrect me, to raise us. You wanted to save us all. But you never did think of asking us if we wanted to be saved, did you, you fuck? No, you didn't, and I should know, because I controlled you, always. You and Palach, all you sick fucks, you don't know shit.

My name is Carl, Juan. Nice to meet you. I work, late nights. A prison. I eat and fart at a desk until dawn, then I come home and sleep and eat and fart at home. My parents are dead. I jerk off with the TV and the Web fuckers. There's pieces of me all over the apartment, turds. I like to keep the heater on, sweaty hot. The screen where these words dance and copulate is smeared, greasy with all kindsa shit. On the keyboard chunky skin flakes, dandruff, snotballs, pizza crumbs, stick out between keys rubbed blank and raw. I type pretty fast. The canary that lies dead in its cage with the grubs, I killed it myself, with my lighter. Hated the noise. The neighbors bitch about the smells, but I hear them fuck and beat each other all the time. Me, I'm quiet. Except my breathing. I breathe loud. The loud rasp of a fat man. It fills the apartment. I fill it. My foul and malodorous spirit.

When I met with Hollis "Kunta Kinte" Mason, he told me I should shower once in while. I told him, "Suck my dick, nigger." That poor Hollis. I played with that boy's mind. The first time I met him, when he was trying to warn "Jan's" "woman friend" from the notebook about "Jan's" "strange behavior," I told him I was a friend of yours, of both of you, and provided enough details from your writings to win his trust. But this time, today, he was suspicious, he didn't know what to think. Poor, dumb porch monkey. He won't ever know shit, either. You're all cut from the same cloth. He just cringed and his eyes bounced back and forth as he gave me the packet with all your letters and old notebook pages and printouts from our chat sessions, all this crap that you kept so carefully in that envelope, in that pathetic apartment filled with clippings and posters of Jan Palach and the book on Tomás Masaryk by Milan Machovec left open on the table, just as Palach left it when he stepped out to fry. That little packet of mementos and keepsakes. You wanted me, you wanted Renée, you wanted Carla, to have it. We thank you. You were real, Juan. Jan. You were real.

.So I write this letter, just for you, so I can print it out and put it together with the other papers and clippings and crap and tie it all up together with a rubber band and then put it in the envelope, so I can burn it. So I can set this last little piece of you on fire too, and watch the ashes fall slowly into my trash can, and disappear. Ashes to ashes. That's what I wanted to tell you. You deserve that. I should know. And one more thing.

I want to be honest with you, Juan. I'm not Carl. I'm not

this is not

this wasn't

this never was

non sono

Ne jestem

nejsem

я не

末じゃやない

我'不是

Ich bin kein

tl hIngan Qo'jIH

non sum

je ne suis pas

no soy

I'm not

Well, never mind what I'm not.

It's over.

Just never you mind.

José Alaniz, professor in the Department of Slavic Languages and Literatures and the Department of Cinema and Media Studies (adjunct) at the University of Washington, Seattle, has published academic books on Russian/Eastern European comics, disability in comics and superheroes. He also writes fiction and makes comics, including for the collections *The Phantom Zone and Other Stories* (Amatl Comix, 2020), *The Compleat Moscow Calling* (Amatl, 2023) and *Puro Pinche True Fictions* (2023, FlowerSong Press). He was born and raised in Edinburg, TX, right in the heart of the Rio Grande Valley.